The Lottery Heiress

ANGELINA ASSANTI

The Lottery Heiress is a work of fiction. The names, characters, places and events are a result of the author's weird imagination. Any resemblance to actual people, places or events is entirely coincidental.

ISBN: 978-0-9979843-0-9

CHAPTER 1

I was already having a bad day. Instead of drinking like I used to, I decided to go shopping. I went to Bloomingdale's and Saks because that's where my peeps go. Did I need to be driving a $200,000 car to an outlet mall? Probably not, but that car makes me feel pretty. After I had dropped a few grand on more stuff I didn't need, I felt like it was time to go.

As I walked to my car, I did what I always do when I drive myself anywhere – I scanned the parking lot for potential threats and saw none. I unlocked the car then threw my small packages on the passenger seat. I sat down and looked around the parking lot one more time and checked myself out in the rear-view mirror.

It was the end of the day, with the sun setting in the pink sky. I decided to go topless - not like college, I meant my convertible. My body stuck to the leather seats as I put my key in the ignition and started the car.

A ferocious roar came from the ten-cylinder engine. As the top disappeared into the trunk, I could see something in my peripheral vision, but by the time I realized what was happening it was too late. I didn't even have time to change from my heels to the moccasins I always wore for driving.

A man came up to the driver's side and stuck a gun in my face. "Get out of the car slowly," he said.

I put my hands in the air. "Look, take it easy, no one needs to get hurt here. Just take whatever you want." I got out of the car and he got in.

"Walk away, quickly," he said. A few seconds later he yelled at me, "Wait."

I turned around, thinking he must've figured out who I was and knew there was a lot more to take than this car.

"I don't know how to drive a stick-shift," he said. And I thought *I* was a poor planner. But I walked back to him because he was the one pointing the gun.

I looked at him in the driver's seat and said nervously, "Look, I'll show you how to drive the car, but please, just throw the gun out of the car, guns *terrify* me." My hands shook slightly.

He thought about it, looked me up and down like he was assessing the danger I posed to him.

I tried to reassure him. "What am I going to do?" I guess I didn't intimidate him because he tossed the gun outside the driver's side window onto the grass curb.

"Open the passenger side door, and I will teach you how to drive this thing," I said. I couldn't believe this *idiot* had actually thrown his gun out of the car. He swung the passenger door out wide.

I walked around to the passenger side, quickly lifted up the bottom of my jeans leg and pulled my .38 Special from my ankle holster. I took the safety off and I held it behind the right side of my body where he couldn't see it. But he looked at my face and could see my countenance had changed.

I was trying not to smirk. I stood at the door opening, keeping my body out of the car so he wouldn't see the gun in my right hand. I pointed with my left hand and said, "Here's what you're going to do. Go ahead and depress the clutch all the way to the floor with your left foot, and with your right hand…" I held up my gun and said, "you're going pick up my phone from the console and call 911."

He sunk his shoulders and picked up my phone. "Come on, I'm on probation," he said.

"Shocker," I said. "I've had a bad day, so you can pick jail or a bullet. *Surprise* me."

He picked up the phone and called 911. "Put it on speaker," I said as I backed away from the car and shut the door with my left hand, never taking the gun off of him.

The operator answered on the first ring. "911, what's your emergency?"

"Hi, I'm being carjacked," I said.

"Where are you right now?" she asked me.

"I'm at the outlet mall in Estero, off I-75."

"What is your name?" she asked.

"Megan Pagano."

"What is the year, make, model and color of your car?"

"It's a 2007 blue Audi R8 GT Spyder. I am parked right in front of the golf store entrance, on the east side."

"And where is the carjacker now?" she asked.

"He's in my car, but I have a gun on him."

I heard a gurgle of laughter over the phone. "And you say he is carjacking *you*?"

"Yes. I told him I was scared of guns and asked him to throw his gun out the window, and he did!"

"Stay on the line with me," she said. "I'm dispatching two units right now."

The carjacker looked at me while he was shaking his head. "I'm going over my minutes for this call. I hope you're happy," I said sarcastically. He just rolled his eyes.

The operator came back on the line. "Can you hear the patrol cars, Megan?"

"Yes, I hear them."

"They will be there in less than a minute. Just stay on the line with me."

"Okay," I said.

"So, is this your boyfriend's car or what?" the carjacker asked.

"No, it's mine."

"What do you do?"

"I'm Megan Pagano."

"Is that name supposed to mean something to me?"

Reluctantly, I told him, "I'm 'The Lottery Heiress.'"

He hit the steering wheel with both hands and gnashed his teeth. "Son of a ...you mean all I had to do was *date* you?" he asked.

Then, I started wiggling the gun. "You said '*no*' to a bullet, right?" I asked bitterly. We stared each other down, and the cops got there just in time, before I had to blink.

The patrol cars came up quickly and screeched to a stop. They drew their weapons on both of us and told me to drop my weapon, which I did. The dispatcher had informed them I was 'The Lottery Heiress' before they got there – that fact always makes people think I'm more charming than I actually am. The first cop arrested the guy and threw him in the back of the patrol car, and then the second cop came over to get my statement. He introduced himself as Officer Daniels.

"So, what happened here?" he asked.

"I was just getting into my car and Mr. Brilliant decides to carjack me, only he can't drive a six-speed so he asks me to come back and give him a lesson," I said.

He laughed. "That is a sweet ride."

"Yeah, thanks," I said.

"So, he came up and put a gun up to you and asked you to get out?" he asked.

"Yeah, then he said 'Wait, I can't drive a standard.'" I said it in a stupid voice, mocking the guy.

The officer continued writing everything down. "Then what happened?"

"Then, I came back and told him guns terrified me and I asked him to throw it out of the car, and he did, so I grabbed my gun out of my ankle holster and had him call you guys on my phone!"

He chuckled and said he was glad I didn't get hurt.

As the investigators were bagging the evidence, Daniels and I walked over to the second officer who was in the driver's seat of his patrol car with the door still open.

Daniels leaned in. "So, Einstein back here decides to carjack 'The Lottery Heiress,' only he's not counting on two things – she's driving a standard and she's packing."

The second cop then turned around to the carjacker and says, "When someone has a license plate frame on their car that says, 'I Heart Smith & Wesson,' you pick another car, idiot."

Daniels added, "You know, you really should've checked the vehicle and made sure you knew how to drive it before you tried to steal it."

Then the other cop looked at me and said, "It's like my dad used to say, 'If you're going to do something stupid, at least be smart about it.'"

I guess the carjacker got tired of being lectured because he shouted, "Can I just go to jail now?"

I guess by now you know from the title of this book that I got my money from the lottery. I guess you think I'm pretty lucky. Well, I'm not, and I would hate for anyone to get money the same way I did. You probably don't believe me, so I'll go back to when it all started – seven years ago. Sometimes it seems much longer than that. Sometimes, it feels like yesterday. But this is all how it began…

★ ★ ★ ★ ★

My mom gave me some really good advice right before I went away to college. She said, "Megan, find out what you love doing and then find a way to get paid for it. That way, you'll feel like you've never worked a day in your life." That was great, except when I got to college I realized I loved two things – men and beer.

And I certainly wasn't the type of girl who would make a living with either men or beer. So I decided to major in Communications and intern at a local radio station. The people at the radio station had great personalities, and most of them had what's described in the business as 'faces for radio.'

People were always surprised I was pretty when they met me in person. This was not a good thing because it began the downward spiral of my radio career. I was getting stalked at the station and when I went to concerts and shows to do promotions, people would stare and point at me.

Some of the men came right up to me, which made me very uncomfortable. I felt like I had to inspect every face in the crowd. I actually had to have a police escort to my car after every show. Not that the cops minded. They were very nice, but I lived in constant fear. Every time I did something simple, like walk to my car or go to the store, I felt I was being watched. When you're being stalked, you look at everyone as a potential threat. The final straw was when a 'fan' assaulted me in the radio station parking lot. I knew I needed to change my career path. And I was determined never to play the victim again.

I went to my academic advisor and asked for some guidance. Since radio was no longer in my future, I knew a change in my major was the only option. I took some Marketing and Public Relations classes and it was a good fit. I would be able to utilize my people skills and my gift of persuasion.

I decided to switch my major to marketing. As I was about to graduate, my political science professor, Dr. Ludlow Palmer, who adored me, asked what my plans were after I graduated. I told him I didn't know. He said he'd spoken to a long-time friend who had a position for me.

It wasn't even an entry-level position. It offered a ridiculous salary and title. Truth be told, I really wasn't qualified to do it right out of college. His buddy from college owned a very successful architecture firm in Miami and needed a marketing and public relations director.

I guess it's true what they say, it's not what you know, it's who you know. It looked as if I was going to get on-the-job training – which is not normal in this field. I know it's not fair, but life is easier when you're cute.

The job was with Mason & Mason, a well-known firm in Miami. It was owned by two brothers. The better known brother, Phillip, had won numerous awards and accolades. He was a rock star of Miami architecture, if you will. Not to mention, he was the good-looking brother.

Phillip was tall, with light brown hair and piercing blue eyes. He had facial hair, which I have never found attractive, and his hair was more than starting to gray. Still, there was something appealing about him. Even though he was quite a bit older than me, he had never married. He was very charming, when he wanted to be.

The firm was well-known on the posh side of Miami. Many of their clients were Wall Street millionaires and celebrities. This job put me in the limelight and I was at the beck and call of some very demanding people. Phillip was a great mentor, though. He respected my opinion and treated me as a peer, which was unusual in this still very male-dominated field.

Phillip's brother Julian, however, was an oddball. He never gave me a second glance, and I always wonder about the ones who don't give *me* a second glance. Clearly, he had issues. He was short, bald and very overweight.

He always wore button-down, long-sleeved shirts that were too small and only one side of the shirt was ever tucked in. And he was a 'sweater.' Not the kind you wear, obviously, the kind you keep your distance from. This is Florida. We are talking about a lot of sweat here.

Even in January when it can dip into the 40s, there he was, still sweating. It was hard to believe these two guys were from the same species, never mind family. Anyway, he didn't have much of a personality. He mumbled a lot and didn't make eye contact, which I didn't like. He also spent a lot of time on the internet. Every time I walked into his office with a question, he panicked. Panicked like a teenager holding a dirty magazine and getting caught by his parents. All I hoped was, whatever he was into wasn't *illegal*.

Phillip and I had several working lunches together. He was extremely professional and made it crystal clear he didn't mix business with pleasure. In fact, we never even had lunch alone. He made it a point never to be alone with any of the women in the office. The scuttlebutt was his attorneys advised him to do this since he was so wealthy. He was a prime target for lawsuits.

From what I understand, sexual harassment refers to *unwanted* advances. Trust me, if he dished it out, no one would complain. Especially his secretary, excuse me, administrative assistant – everyone gets so offended nowadays. Anyway, I didn't like her at all. She was useless. Her name was Melinda and she couldn't even take a message properly.

The only thing she did do well was make Phillip's coffee the way he liked it, and tell him how good he looked or how brilliant he was. Ugh. She made me crazy. And it wasn't only me. She annoyed all the women in the office. The guys in the office liked her though. She was cute – I guess, in a way, for a piranha.

The most ridiculous thing she did was talk in this really high-pitched voice and giggle when she was with Phillip, but around the women in the office she had a totally different voice. I mean, when she spoke and moved her mouth, it looked as if she was being dubbed.

I wondered if Phillip caught on to any of that…

probably not. She wore very low cut shirts and men get easily distracted around cleavage. Even a well-educated man, trying to stay away from litigation, gets distracted. What she didn't have from her neck up, she worked from her neck down. People may not like me, but at least what you see is what you get. If there's one thing I can't stand, it's a phony!

I was pretty bored with my social life up to this point. Don't get me wrong, I had plenty of men around. I enjoyed them and discarded them when I was done. Most of my friends were married, but I was still going out almost every night. It was fun for a while, but when my friends started having kids, then I thought maybe it was time to get serious.

Was I ready for serious? I was in my early twenties, was there so much more to learn about life? I was about to find out.

I'll never forget the day Phillip came into my office with a concerned look on his face. It was right before the 4th of July. He let everyone else in the office go home early – except me. Phillip had been selected to design a building considered too contemporary for the location and the community was lashing out at the firm.

It was, after all, a Mediterranean-style area, and the architecture of the surrounding businesses and homes reflected that. Even Wal-Mart was forced to use certain colors and building designs in the area.

"Megan, where are we with the Westman building?" he asked, while throwing a huge file on my desk.

"I just contacted the mayor this morning," I told him, "I still haven't heard back from his people. And I can't plan a press conference with comments from the mayor when he won't return my calls."

"Why don't you cruise down to his office and use your feminine wiles to get what we need?"

"Nice," I said as I looked him up and down. At least he realized I was a woman. He never acknowledged that before. I loved the way his blue shirt brought out the steel gray flecks in his eyes. It was getting harder and harder to pretend I didn't want him.

"Listen, Megan, this thing is going to get worse and worse without his support. His hesitation is going to cause a public relations nightmare for the firm." He came closer and closer to me with every sentence.

"So, what am I supposed to do?" I asked him, as I backed up against my desk. He was almost on top of me. He came into my personal space and almost whispered in my ear.

"Get the mayor's support and then convince the community this is in their best interest." He backed up and looked at me longingly, still not realizing he was too close.

"It's an election year," I reminded him, trying not to let him hear my heart pounding harder and harder. I felt myself arching my back to avoid brushing his skin.

"Then remind people this company is bringing a thousand jobs to the area. Honestly, I think you're losing your touch." He put his hands around me, and touched my desk. I thought he was going to kiss me. My breathing became rapid.

"The people in this community hate the design of the building. They're ready to chase you with pitchforks and torches."

"Then hold an informational meeting. Explain the fact

this is a technology firm and they *need* to have a contemporary design." He touched the pendant I was wearing and rested his hand over it. I looked down at his hand. He pulled it away, finally realizing how inappropriately he was behaving.

"It would be nice if you attended one of these meetings for a change, since I'm not an architect," I said as I fanned myself with the file I was holding.

"Fine, schedule it."

"Really?" I asked.

"Yeah, I don't need you on my case, too. And since you're heading downtown anyway, I need you to bring this CD and the plan revisions to Mark Taylor." He casually tossed the CD across my desk.

Now, Mark Taylor was a Hollywood bad boy. He was in Miami shooting the action thriller *Don O'Malley*. He had purchased an old Mediterranean house and hired Phillip to do the renovations. I hadn't met Mr. Taylor, but some of my co-workers had, and they said he was most unpleasant. I wasn't surprised because every time I was at the grocery store, Mark Taylor's face would be on some tabloid magazine's cover.

The headlines always involved his public drunkenness, him punching a photographer, or pictures of him and his flavor of the month. I found him repulsive and I did not appreciate the idea of being alone with him, even just for a few minutes.

I've been around many powerful and wealthy men. In my experience, they are used to getting what they want. I know stars always claim you can't believe what they write in these magazines. But how can so many articles be wrong?

I got up and put the CD and other materials in my

portfolio. "Why can't your assistant drop these off?" I asked.

He smiled at me. "Because Mark specifically asked for my prettiest employee."

"Really?" I was delighted Phillip thought I was the prettiest.

"Unfortunately, Maria is on vacation, so I need you to do it," he said, smiling.

"Well, the joke's on you because I can't wait to meet him!" I said sarcastically.

"Be careful; he's going to hit on you." He looked me up and down. "And in that outfit, you're asking for trouble from any man."

"What's wrong with this? It goes down to my knees and it's not even tight."

"No, but it shows off your silhouette." He stood next to me and outlined the sides of my body, without once touching me.

"What are you doing?" I asked him.

"I don't know." Phillip said. He sounded embarrassed.

"Well, I'm going to go now." I said. He leaned in with some hesitation. He looked torn. Maybe he too, was trying to decide if this was worth the risk. I stood there for a few seconds, I don't know why – maybe I was waiting for a kiss that didn't come. I just looked at him. I grabbed my purse and picked up my portfolio.

He turned away. "Have a good weekend, Megan."

"Yeah, you too," I said, wondering what I was in for. I was not looking forward to this meeting.

The distance to Mark Taylor's house wasn't far. The traffic was smooth and I drove fast in my Mustang convertible. I liked the wind blowing in my hair and on my face. I didn't care about how I looked when I got there. Besides, I had only one thing on my mind – Phillip. I couldn't stop analyzing his behavior. I knew I was one of the only single people in the office, but I didn't have the best reputation when it came to dating.

So what if I liked beer, chicken wings and basketball? It wasn't my idea to watch the Miami Heat game at Hooters one night with my ex. And, that's when I had an epiphany. It was the perfect place to dump my boyfriends – if they took it badly, I could just point and say, "Look, boobs," and I knew they'd be okay.

I probably shouldn't have shared this story with my co-workers, but I did find it amusing, as did they. And, really, by no fault of my own, Hooters became the place where my relationships went to *die*. I knew Phillip had heard of this practice, affectionately referred to as the 'Hooters Kiss of Death' and that's why I was so surprised by Phillip's sudden interest in me.

I was trying to find Mark's house in a neighborhood I didn't even know existed. The houses were beautiful. They were old Florida mansions. With all the yachts, golf courses and fancy restaurants, it was easy to see it was an area for the rich and famous. I got to his house and just sat in my car, staring.

He had a 1920s Mediterranean home and was trying to keep the integrity of the home without a lot of modern touches. It was beautiful. It was basically my dream house. I loved the pale yellow color contrasting with the big red roof tiles and wrought iron. It had the original doors, windows, shutters and fixtures. Of course the landscaping was perfect. I muttered, "Lord, why can't I live here?" I tried not to be bitter and jealous. I failed.

I carried the plans to the door across the brick pavers that tied this picture perfect property together. No one answered the door. I knocked again, and again. I decided not to lug the plans around to the back door.

I walked through a breezeway that framed a view of the Intracoastal Waterway. There was a huge water fountain, like something you'd expect to see in Italy, spilling success off of every tier. The pool was the color of a tropical ocean far away from the chaos of Miami.

This was my dream house and it belongs to a violent, womanizing, drunkard. So unfair. I looked around the backyard and took in the view, almost forgetting what I was doing there. The water was so beautiful, and quiet, and serene. It was hard to believe I was in the middle of Miami.

With a sigh of envy, I knocked on the back door. But it wasn't latched, and opened with the touch of my hand. I looked inside. I cautiously stepped into a gorgeous gourmet kitchen. I bet he didn't even know how to cook.

"Mr. Taylor? I'm from Phillip Mason's office. I have your plans." I started to explore his house further, when I noticed him in the living room, just steps away from the kitchen. He was lying on the floor in front of the sofa and it didn't even look as if he was breathing. Around him were enough empty bottles to sing that old song. "Mr. Taylor? Mr. Taylor!" I gently slapped his face and turned his head.

Just enough, apparently, to make him feel it was the time to barf everything he ate since childhood right onto the Gucci dress and shoes I had bought the week before. I was thrown into a violent storm of dry heaving. I jumped to my feet, reached for my phone, and called 911. I kept coughing and gagging as I waited for them to arrive. I decided I would never tell anyone about this. I'd figure out how to have Mark sign the plan revisions later.

★ ★ ★ ★ ★

The firemen and the EMTs were real chatty. Maybe they got off on the novelty of rescuing an alcohol-poisoned celebrity, but all I wanted to do was take a shower.

The guy taking his vitals was named Chuck. He looked at me, "You his girlfriend?"

Disgusting. "No! I'm just here dropping off plans for his renovation," I said looking at Mark who was coming in and out of consciousness.

"Good thing you showed up when you did, he almost pulled a Jimi Hendrix."

"Lucky me," I said sarcastically.

"Does he have any family here?" he asked.

"I have no idea. I can try and find his phone. But I'd like to get in the shower. I am not driving home like this."

"I understand," he said, and he smiled. Was he really flirting with me while I was covered in vomit? I patted Mark down for his house keys and found them in his pocket. Chuck raised his eyebrows at me.

"What, should I have bought him dinner first?" I was feeling really snarky. I called Phillip and told him what happened. He told me to lock the house and take the keys.

They started to put Mark on the gurney and wheel him out. "It was nice meeting you."

"Yup," I said over my shoulder as I looked around for the master bedroom.

"Is there a number we can get to contact you about his condition?"

"Look, I'm covered in vomit right now. I couldn't care

less about him."

"Man, you are pathetic," the other EMT said to Chuck as they wheeled Mr. Taylor out the door. I locked the door behind them and went to clean up.

I found the bedroom. I'd never been in a man's bedroom alone. And I would *never* be in this man's bedroom. I looked around. I liked the furniture. He had a really large mirror on one wall, no doubt to stare at himself. It was a very impersonal room. No paintings and no pictures.

I went into his closet. Of course, all the clothes were designer clothes. But, he was tall and nothing fit me. I opened his dresser drawer, grabbed a pair of sweatpants and a t-shirt. I took my clothes off and stepped into the shower.

It had this tall shower system that looked like it could beam me up somewhere. Rich people are so weird. I looked around to see if he had cameras in the bathroom. He just seemed kind of freaky. Well, I mean, the little I have read about him. I got out of the shower and quickly wrapped a towel around me. I dried off and got dressed, wondering why someone would drink so much. Alone, no less. He must really hate himself.

I looked in the mirror. I looked really stupid in Mark Taylor's t-shirt and huge sweatpants. They were practically falling off. I remember they smelled like lilac detergent. I *hate* lilac. What kind of guy would want to walk around smelling like flowers?

I drove home and called the hospital and made sure Barfy didn't die, but I was not impressed. I never wanted to see him again.

I was on my way to take another shower when I heard a knock at the door. Then I heard the doorbell ring. Then

I heard both at the same time.

"Hold your dang horses," I yelled as I put on my bathrobe. Who on earth would be bothering me when I am trying to rinse the smell of puke out of my nose? I flung open the door, all ready to let someone have it, and there was Phillip Mason standing in my doorway.

"Hi," he said, "I just came to get the keys."

"Oh, sure, they're in my purse. Come on in." He walked in to my condo.

"Megan, I am so sorry. I blame myself for sending you there."

"It's not your fault. But I probably won't eat for a week."

"Too bad, I came to see if you wanted to have dinner."

"Are you sure that's wise?"

"No!" he said with a huge smile and a twinkle in his eye.

"Where do you want to go?"

"Anywhere but Hooters," he said with a devilish grin.

"Give me a couple of minutes to get dressed."

A few minutes went by. I wasn't sure how to dress. If I wore something too conservative, maybe he wouldn't know I was interested. I didn't want to send the wrong message by wearing something sleazy. I just decided to wear a low cut shirt with a mini skirt and peep toe shoes. I wanted him, and I wasn't going to hide it anymore. I got barfed on today, I needed to be kissed – kissed long and hard.

We went to a popular Asian fusion restaurant. It had the best food! I felt a little weird about having dinner with the boss. Before today, he was always extremely professional and reserved, but he sure didn't seem that way at dinner. I knew this wasn't a 'date' but he was looking awfully interested.

He took a big gulp of his beer. "What are you thinking right now?"

"I plead the fifth."

"C'mon," he prodded.

"Honestly, I am wondering why we're having dinner. You realize I never got to the mayor's office?" I sat back in my chair.

"We can talk about that later. We have to eat, right?"

I took a swig of my beer and looked him straight in the face. "Is this more than dinner? You don't normally wear cologne."

"It's just dinner between colleagues," he insisted.

I leaned forward. "If I didn't work for you, would we be here right now?"

He leaned in and said, "If you didn't work for me, we'd be back at my place right now."

I raised my eyebrows and sat back in my seat. "That is extremely presumptuous of you." I stroked my pilsner glass. "I'm not looking for a fling, okay? I love working for you. And when things go south, because they *will*, then I'm out of a job."

"Look, I don't know where this is going, Megan, but I know I want to be with you, and I wouldn't be saying this except I think you want it too." Oh, he was so confident.

I scoffed at him. "I'm in love with Julian," I confessed.

"Oh, why don't women notice me instead of him?" he said, pretending to be serious.

"We like a challenge!"

He laughed and excused himself to the restroom.

The waiter dropped off the check. "Will there be anything else for you this evening?"

There was no one around and I needed some helpful

words from someone. I gestured to the chair Phillip was in.

"This man is my boss, and he wants to be more. How do I know if he's worth losing my job over?" I asked the waiter.

"See how he tips."

I laughed.

"I'm serious. You can tell a lot about a person by the way they tip."

He looked at Phillip walking towards the table and then back at me. "Good luck." He picked up our plates and walked away.

"You ready?" Phillip asked as he pulled out his wallet and picked up the check.

Phillip paid the bill. I tried to peek at the tip but I couldn't see what he wrote. We walked out to his Porsche and he opened the door for me. I hate power locks; no one opens doors for you anymore. But he did, so I figured he had other intentions. And I was right, because he kissed me right there. We started driving back to my condo. I looked down at my hand in his, thinking what a mess I had gotten myself into.

"Are you okay with this?"

"Okay with what?" I was trying to play it cool. But I definitely didn't want him to see anyone else. I had been working for this guy for over a year. And I was sick of all the women in the office drooling over him and touching him when they spoke to him.

"Okay with us," he said.

"What do you mean?"

"I mean, I want to be with you and I would go crazy if I had to share you."

"Wow. After one kiss, you decided that?" I was

stunned. He was the most eligible bachelor in Miami. No, really, it was in the newspaper and a local business magazine. And he wanted to be with me. I couldn't blame him. I am adorable, but still… I work for this guy.

He signs my paychecks. What happens if things go bad? The Architecture field is very small. You meet the same people over and over again. And, everyone will think I slept my way to this position. There is so much at stake here.

"Megan, I knew when I met you a year ago I wanted to be with you."

"Me too," I said.

He smiled, "Really?"

"Yeah, I can always tell when someone wants me."

"Very funny. I just thought the age difference was going to be too much."

"You're not that much older."

"You know I don't date people who work for me, so we need to keep this quiet."

"I don't think I want people to know either, Phillip. Everyone at the office will start acting…*weirder*."

Phillip pulled into my subdivision and turned the car off. He pulled his keys out of the ignition, "Can I come in if I promise to be a gentleman?"

I turned to him, "If you're going to be a gentleman, don't *bother* coming in," I said as I got out of the car. I shut his door and walked up to the door to my house. He bounced up the stairs before I could even get the door open.

We dated for about a year before we got engaged. Eventually we told everyone at the firm. It was kind of hard to keep our impending marriage a secret. My parents were thrilled. They wanted grandchildren – that's usually all they talked about when I brought up the wedding, and that's all they talked to Phillip about. But it seemed he wanted kids just as much as they wanted us to have them.

Phillip was great. We even started to write our own vows because he couldn't find any that expressed how crazy he was for me. He seemed perfect and he always knew how to make me laugh. I didn't know how life could get any better. Phillip was everything I ever wanted in a man.

CHAPTER 2

Then the pains started. And they did not go away. I went to several doctors and no one could figure out what was wrong. Finally, a young doctor doing his residency at Miami General Hospital told me he thought I had endometriosis but the only way to find out for sure was to have surgery. So I had the surgery and Phillip was there through everything. Then we got the news.

The doctor sat us down and explained it would be nearly impossible for me to conceive. I took the news fine. I didn't think I wanted children anyway. But that was just the first blow in a series of horrible events. The car ride home was not fun. There was dead silence. And Phillip was a talker, like me. So silence was clearly not a good sign.

"What's the matter?" I asked. "I'm the one that has to deal with the diagnosis."

"I just… I just wasn't expecting this."

"Well, it's not like I knew I couldn't have rug rats."

"Megan, can you be serious? I can't have a serious conversation with you?" he said, slamming his hands on the steering wheel.

"You can try," I said, "but I feel like it's going to be very one-sided."

"See, you always do this."

"What?"

"You have to make a joke out of everything. Why can't you be serious about something that will end our relationship?"

"Oh, you're not going to marry me now?"

"Not if you can't have my kids!"

"Wow. You're dumping me because I can't get knocked up?"

"I'm pretty sure you don't call it being 'knocked up' if you're married to the person."

"Well, I would."

"I just need to find someone fertile to carry on my name."

My pale skin was turning red with anger. "With all of my character flaws, you pick on my eggs? You bastard!"

"I'm older than you. You know I wanted to have kids right away."

"What do you want me to do? I *can't* have kids."

"Then I guess there's nothing left to discuss."

"Hey, let's not forget, things weren't working on your end either, but I can't take a pill to fix my problem."

"You said you'd never mention that!"

"I just did!"

We got to my house and slammed both the car doors. He announced he would be taking all of his stuff. I offered to help him pack to get him out faster. I didn't even want to look at him anymore. Phillip and I never even had an argument before. Yet he was willing to leave me that quickly. Better before the wedding than after, I guess.

While Phillip and I were screaming at each other, and throwing random items into a cardboard box, my parents were a hundred miles away. My cell phone was ringing at the same time as the house phone. I picked up my cell phone.

It was one of my mom and dad's closest friends, Carol. She ran the diner my parents owned at the beach. I felt hot. Warm tears ran down my cheeks and I remember I couldn't hear anything. Phillip knew there was something wrong and dropped his box and he came over to hold me.

"What happened?"

"My parents were in an accident."

"Are they okay?" he asked.

"I'm not sure. Carol said they're dead." I was in shock and clearly, not making any sense.

Carol told me some selfish moron was texting while driving and ran right through a red light and t-boned my parents' car. Of course, that idiot walked away with no injuries.

Phillip just held me and he kept saying how sorry he was. I wondered if he meant because he dumped me or because my parents had died. I let him hold me and then I went to the kitchen and took one of the pills my doctor gave me after the surgery. It's funny, I didn't need them after the surgery, but I didn't feel this much pain then.

My parents lived in Fort Myers, which was on the west coast, about two hours from Miami. He offered to drive me there and I let him. As far as I was concerned, he owed me, and I was in no condition to drive. Especially after popping a second pill after we started driving.

I wondered how I was going to handle everything. I never coped with things very well. Now I was going to face all those people at the funeral and what? Pretend everything was great with Phillip and me? I was just going through the motions at this point. I didn't want to talk about Phillip. Plus, I didn't know what kind of arrangements my parents had made. We never talked about it.

I wondered how much money the funeral was going to cost and then I felt bad I was worrying about money when I lost the only two people who ever loved me just as I was. There were so many thoughts racing through my head. They'll never see me get married. They'll never see their grandchildren – oops, I forgot, I can scratch that off the list. There are so many things I didn't get to tell them. And I hadn't made the time to get to Fort Myers and visit.

There really was no excuse except the fact they didn't want Phillip and me sleeping in the same bed until we were married. Who cares? Why did I make such a big deal out of that? Now, I would never see them again. For what? Not being able to sleep in the same bed as my fiancé who dumped me anyway? I was so ashamed. I was so sorry.

The funeral is a faded memory, except for the hugging. I am not a hugger. In fact, I would be happy never to hug anyone again. I popped pain meds all weekend. Truthfully, I was like a zombie, but with better hair. I couldn't have gotten through it without Carol's support. I was so glad she was there.

Phillip was useless. His younger brother lived in Fort Myers, so he went to visit him. Why did I not see any of this coming? I shouldn't have let him drive me here. I'd made a mistake. It didn't feel right having him stay in this house with me. Nothing felt right anymore. Carol wouldn't stop nagging me about going to my parents' attorney's office. And he kept calling me and telling me it was urgent I settle my parent's affairs. How could I? I couldn't even control my own life.

After a few days, I convinced Phillip he should go back to Miami. I didn't want to prolong the inevitable. He didn't want to marry me and I didn't want to marry someone who ran when things get tough. He was no help to me anyway.

I had about thirty grand in the bank. I could take a few weeks off without worrying about my job situation. I didn't know what would happen to me. I knew I couldn't go back to working for Phillip. At best, I hoped he would at least give me a good recommendation so I could work somewhere else. Now, I had the difficult task of going through my parents' stuff, deciding what to keep, what to toss and what to donate.

I found and played my parents' old Beatles records and I stopped dead when "Let It Be" came on the record player. I had heard that song a thousand times before and never listened to the words. Now, I am not a spiritual person, but when the chorus came on, I felt like I was surrounded by angels. It brought some strange comfort to me. There I was, sorting through sixty years of memories, deciding which ones to keep. I couldn't do it. There was a lot I couldn't do.

Carol came over unannounced. I opened the door. "Hi Carol."

She came in. "How are you holding up, honey?"

"I've been drinking…a lot."

"Well, that's not good." She looked around. There

were piles of stuff everywhere. "You're sure you don't want help?"

"No, I just want to be alone."

"All right, all I ask is you let me drive you down to your attorney."

"I don't have an attorney."

"You do now, and you can't put this off anymore."

"If I go, they're...you know," I said with a tear rolling off my face.

"Honey, they're gone – no matter what." She hugged me and she had tears in her eyes too.

"I'm going to get dressed." And then I thought no one walks into a law office without an appointment. "Don't we need to make an appointment?" I asked.

"Trust me; they'll drop what they're doing."

I don't have a lot of regrets in my life, but I never got to say goodbye to my parents, and it still hurts. And, I was racked with guilt. I found myself hoping they didn't owe money on their house or car or the diner – that *stupid* diner they opened on the beach. I had been after them to sell because they made no money in the summer when the snowbirds were gone. But they refused. They said it was like a big family.

The same employees and customers had been there for years. The locals relied on it. It had become sort of a landmark. The name of it was Big Mama's and the sign had a fat lady holding a pig with a beach scene in the background.

Dad's Corvette was always parked in the front of the building. People always knew when he was at the diner. He had become good friends with many of the locals, and the snowbirds enjoyed coming back every winter to hear what exciting things were going on in the area.

I let Carol drive me to the attorney's office. She said she didn't think I should drive. I didn't see what the big deal was but I didn't feel like arguing about something so stupid. We took McGregor Boulevard to West First Street in downtown Fort Myers. There must be hundreds of palm trees on McGregor. I never really noticed how many there were when I drove myself.

The office building was very pretty. It was three stories and had pillars on the outside. It looked like their clients were well-to-do. Begrudgingly, I walked into the attorney's office. As soon as we got there, we were whisked away, given bottled water and shown to a room filled with muffins and other simple carbs. I looked around at the full sized floor-to-ceiling windows, the silk drapes and the granite floors and was convinced my parents were getting hosed by this attorney. What was this guy's hourly rate?

We were brought to James Buchanan's executive office and he showed up almost immediately, unusual for someone who bills by the hour. He said, "Hey, I am so glad to meet you." He extended his hand and gave Carol a kiss on the check. He gestured for us to sit in the chairs in front of his desk. He sat down and clasped his hands.

"Wow. You're really pretty," he said.

"Wow, you're really inappropriate," I replied.

"Sorry, I'm just thinking about a pretty girl like you with all that money." I ignored his comment. "So, 'The Lottery Heiress' has come home. Your mom and dad – great people, I was so sorry to hear about the way…"

I interrupted. "I think there's been a mistake. I am here for Shannon and Anthony Pagano's will."

"Right, I've got your file right here. Imagine winning all that lottery money and barely getting to enjoy it," he said.

"Uh, I think your files are mixed up. My parents never won the lottery."

He looked at me. Then he looked at Carol.

"If my parents won the lottery, I think I'd know, and she would know," I said smugly as I looked at Carol.

She gave me an apologetic look. "I'm sorry, honey. They made us all promise not to say anything." I looked at her, horrified. She defended herself. "I mean, you were going to find out in a few months anyway. They set up a trust for you when you turn 25." I sat back in my chair and exhaled. Mr. Buchanan gave me a sympathetic look.

"My parents won the lottery and didn't tell me?" I clenched my fists and grunted. I sat forward again and started flailing my arms in disgust. "How could they not tell me? They acted like they were struggling. I was sending them money. They must've thought it was real funny. I was sending them money!"

I took a deep breath, sat back again and asked Mr. Buchanan, "How much did they leave, exactly?"

He opened the file on his desk and pointed, "At the close of the stock market yesterday, that number right there."

"Is that my account number?" I asked. He laughed. Carol laughed. I did not laugh.

"No, that's your net worth." He was still laughing. "Account number. That's priceless."

I took a closer look at the number. I started to count the digits. My eyes widened. "Holy crap." I tried to process everything being said to me.

"Your parents hit the interstate power play jackpot." Then he asked Carol casually, "How many weeks did that thing roll over?"

"I think it was a couple of months," she answered.

"Of course," he continued, "this figure changes on a daily basis with interest, the stock market, and your assets. All these things contribute. But the fact is you're set for the rest of your life. Heck, your grandchildren are all set," he said with a game show host smile.

I got up and I felt both lightheaded and relieved at the same time. "Excuse me," I said as I walked out into the hall. For the first time since my parents died, I felt okay. The money meant I'd never have to lay eyes on Phillip again. I would never have to go back to Miami. And I would never have to work again. I didn't have my parents, but I had the security of knowing I could do whatever I wanted.

I called Phillip. He didn't answer his cell phone so I left him a message. "Hi Phillip. It's Megan. I am changing my status from 'leave of absence' to 'retirement' effective immediately. Thanks."

I spent a long time signing papers and getting smiles from everyone in the office who clearly knew I was 'The Lottery Heiress.' I hated that title, yet I would see it used countless times in the local newspaper. You would think people would want to give me sympathy, but you know, most of them just told me why I should give them money. I couldn't believe how much being a millionaire changed my life. And it wasn't for the better.

It was a quiet ride back to my parents' house.

"Are you mad at me?" Carol asked.

"No. My parents asked you not to tell me. I'm glad you respected their wishes. I just wish they had told me."

"They were trying to protect you, Megan. They knew people would bother you and act different around you if they knew you were a millionaire."

"I can't believe they didn't tell me."

"They were worried you might go a little nuts with the money."

"C'mon, that's ridiculous. Phillip's a millionaire. I'm used to being around money."

"Money has a way of changing people and they were just afraid…"

"Maybe I would have made different decisions if I had known."

"What do you mean?"

"I don't know, maybe I knew Phillip wasn't the one and I ignored it," I said as I looked at the palm trees whizzing by.

"You were having doubts about Phillip?"

"I think so. He's old money, you know? I enjoyed the lifestyle. I liked the vacations, the private jets, the expensive cars. Maybe I would've made different decisions. Maybe I would've moved to Fort Myers if I knew I didn't have much time left with them. Maybe they wouldn't have had an accident at all if I had been there."

"Maybe. But maybe you would've been in the car, too. Megan, things happen the way they happen. You have to accept it, and you can't blame yourself. You weren't the one responsible."

We didn't talk much after that conversation. She just dropped me off at the house and I told her I'd be by the diner later.

I went back to cleaning out my parents' house. It was awful. Looking back, I should've asked friends to help. But I wanted to be alone. I got to the kitchen cabinets and opened the liquor cabinet and mixed myself a drink, then spit it out. Hard liquor never tasted good to me. I dumped all the bottles down the sink.

I was eating a sandwich some time later, listening to more of their old records, and I grabbed one of Dad's beers from the fridge. I hate to say it, but the first bottle went down pretty easily. The fourth and fifth went down even easier.

★ ★ ★ ★ ★

I woke up at 4:00 in the morning to the sound of a record skipping. My head was pounding. I took two Advil with a half-empty bottle of beer from the night before. Somehow I pressed on. I continued cleaning. I just wanted to be done with it.

By this time, I was trying to figure out where I wanted to go. Should I sell my condo in Miami? I decided to keep my parents' house in Fort Myers. It was on the Orange River. It is one of the most populated manatee hangouts. It's near a power plant, which means the water is always warm for the sea cows. I loved going out to the dock with my morning coffee and seeing hundreds of manatee eating barnacles off of my dock. I knew I had to keep the river house.

I decided I would sell the house in Fort Myers Beach. It was a nice house but it was accessible to the average beach-goer, and now that I had money, as a single woman, I needed to think about my safety. I decided I would buy my own dream house on the beach.

I'd made the decision about where I'd live, but I was so confused about everything else. And the sad part was I didn't have any friends who offered any insight or real wisdom. My friends suggested I see the world, but the world is full of bad people. You'd have to be crazy to think it's wise for an attractive single millionaire to travel by herself. Even my best friend, Cindy, had bad advice.

She told me to just go shopping and I would feel better. That was just a temporary fix, like everything else. My parents were gone. I don't know why she thought going to Banana Republic would cheer me up. She said she meant like Worth Ave. shopping in Palm Beach. She always did have champagne taste; at least she had a champagne budget to match. Her husband was an executive for a Fortune 500 company.

About a month after the accident, I decided I would occupy myself by looking for a house on the beach. I also decided to sell my condo. I was not going back to Miami. I didn't want to read in the paper how Phillip's future wife birthed a whole soccer team. I cried, "Oh, God, why does this stuff have to happen?" But he didn't answer.

It seemed like the medical bills didn't stop coming. I always hated paying bills, but the worst part of this thing was paying the hospital and doctors' bills for people who died anyway. You never think about it until it happens to you. How do people make it through this life? I guess if you have someone by your side, someone you can count on, it would be easier. I didn't have Phillip, I didn't have my parents and I sure didn't have someone who knew what it was like to have millions of dollars.

I never felt so alone. I was almost ready to put their beach house on the market when I stumbled across some old boxes in the crawl space. I went through one of the boxes and found my old gown, sash and crown from when I was Ms. Juicy Citrus 2004. I got a bottle of champagne out of the wine cooler, popped the cork and tried on my old stuff. I couldn't get the zipper up.

There was a picture of me at the pageant with my parents. I stood for a long time with that picture in one hand and a half-empty bottle of Dom Perignon in the other. I looked in a mirror, put my finger in my mouth and pointed to a tooth in back and cried, "This is the only crown I have now." I laughed hysterically, and cried for hours.

I woke up to someone banging on my door. I must've passed out. It was the next day. I passed a mirror in the hallway and got a gander at myself. My make-up was smeared and I had a faint outline of where my lipstick donned my mouth. I didn't look like a beauty queen anymore.

I answered the door in my half-zipped gown, crown and sash.

Thank God it was just Carol. "Well, hello, your highness. I would curtsy but I threw my back out again."

"Ha ha. What do you want?"

"I came to check on you," she said "Everyone at the diner is worried about you."

"They just want to know if I'm closing the diner. Don't feed me your bull about people caring about me."

"Megan, I care about you. You've been in self-destruct mode since your parents' accident. I think you need to come down to the diner and get out of the house."

"Fine. But I need to shower and get dressed first."

"I think you should send that dress to the dry cleaner."

"I'm going to donate it. I think all this humidity shrank it."

"Yeah, the humidity," she rolled her eyes.

After I cleaned myself up, I grabbed the keys to Dad's '63 Z06 Corvette and drove to Big Mama's to inform everyone I would be selling it. What would I do with a diner? I had no idea how to run one. I didn't need to justify it to anyone. I was definitely selling.

When I walked in, the smell of old grease backhanded

me in the face. I looked around at the old, red and white, chipped linoleum flooring and stained checkered curtains. The tables had Formica peeling up on the corners, the chrome stools at the counter had the foam exposed on the them and the ceiling tiles that weren't missing, were stained. Why would anyone eat here? Why would millionaires let this diner fall into such disrepair? I was totally embarrassed to own this dump. I mean, even though it's just a crappy little diner, it *is* right on the ocean!

Everyone seemed sincerely glad to see me. I hadn't seen some of those characters in years. There was Bud, a retired Green Beret, who was a customer and a permanent fixture at the diner. He didn't look like much, but I heard he could really kick some butt.

There were always different line cooks I couldn't keep track of. And occasionally, we had Eddy, a developmentally disabled guy, help bus tables. He only worked a few hours a week. He lived in a group home and he found some independence through working.

Then there was Mary, a brutally honest lady from the Florida panhandle. She was dark-skinned, but when people labeled her as African-American she let them know her family was from the islands, not Africa. She wore really bright clothes, as loud as her personality, and she was always good for a laugh. Like me, she is bold and sometimes speaks without thinking about what she's going to say. Somehow it seems less offensive with a little southern accent. She was a widow and her only son died in Afghanistan.

Amy was my age. She started there right after high school. She had young kids and was the type who just wanted to settle down, but couldn't seem to find the right guy. She was a serial hugger, and perpetually in love, just with different people.

Of course there was Carol. Thank God for her. She kept the diner running and helped keep me together after this whole mess happened. I thought about it. Why should I sell the place? I was taking time off from my career.

I had decided to leave everyone I knew behind in Miami, including my best friend, and live in my parents' house. Maybe I shouldn't sell the diner and put all of those people out of work. Who cares if it doesn't turn a profit? Suddenly I understood why Dad kept this place. I knew the first order of business was to renovate.

I laid a hand on Eddy's shoulder and took a step forward. "I'm sure you're all wondering what my plans are for the diner. I know you think I don't care about you or Big Mama's. But, I feel like I know each one of you. I know it's not possible, but it feels like my parents are still here somehow. And they cared for you all so much – I'd be disappointing them if I sold this place. So, as long as this place is standing, you all will have a job here."

Amy came over and hugged me. "So long as no one ever hugs me again," I added. They all laughed, as though I'd made a joke. Then Carol came over and thanked me and everyone else did too. Had I made the right choice? I announced I would be closing the diner for a complete renovation, and they would all be paid for the time off during the renovation. I contacted a local contractor and turned the job over to Carol.

I told Carol I needed to go to The Ritz-Carlton in Naples to learn how to be wealthy. I'd dated plenty of wealthy men, but it's different when it's your own money. You have the control, you make the decisions. I got in my Corvette and made the 45-minute drive to the hotel.

When I pulled up under the portico, I realized I'd forgotten to pack anything! I let the valet take my car and checked into the nicest room they had, which was the Presidential Suite. I went over to the window and looked out over the ocean, wondering if my parents had a clue how screwed up I had become. I wondered how Phillip was doing. And I wondered how on earth I was going to function.

Well, I wasn't helping myself by standing there. So I went to the concierge and asked for a limo. You can do that at places like the Ritz. I just asked for one and 'poof,' there it was. I had the driver take me down Tamiami Trail to 5th Ave. I liked the west coast. There are so many millionaires in Naples. I seriously considered buying a house there so I could be among people I had things in common with. In fact, I sent for a real estate agent to show me some properties in the area.

But as the week at the hotel escaped from me, I realized I was more alone here than in Fort Myers. I looked around. It felt as though I was the only single person there. Some vacationers were honeymooners, some were business travelers and others were families. I was sure none were in my situation. I ate dinner by myself at all the restaurants.

I felt like everyone was staring at me because I was alone. I watched the children walking with their parents, laughing and causing mischief. Then I watched the families with one parent on the phone, while the other was yelling at their kids and their nannies – those must be fun households to grow up in. Finally, I watched the couples in love. Even the miserable people had company.

So I did the only thing that made sense at the time. I went home to Fort Myers.

I didn't even unpack my new things. I ordered a pizza and opened a beer and plopped down in front of the television. I saw a commercial for Audi on television. The people in the ad looked so happy. I wondered if I would be happy if I had an Audi. I was watching way too much TV. I was isolating myself because everywhere I went, people knew I was rich. And they were asking me for money like crazy. I got about 20 letters a day from people asking for money. I decided two things; I would hire someone to sort through my mail and I was going to buy an Audi.

I drove my Mustang to the dealership. I was just going to buy a little convertible. It was only sixty grand. Then I made the mistake of asking if they had any six-speeds. I knew I couldn't control a lot in my life, but at least I could control a car.

The salesman showed me an R8 GT Spyder in the showroom. It was blue and had beige leather that was so soft, it was like touching suede. It was the only car on the lot that wasn't an automatic. He said, "It's a hundred and eighty grand. Someone ordered it and then changed their mind."

"I want to test drive it."

He laughed. Then he noticed I wasn't laughing. "You're serious? How are *you* planning to pay for that?" He asked with a condescending tone.

"I'm Megan Pagano," I said as I clicked my tongue and folded my arms.

"Have we met?" he asked sarcastically.

"You wish! I'm 'The Lottery Heiress.' Now, go get the keys." I said with a major attitude.

He practically ran to get the keys. He had to have other employees move other cars around to get it out of the showroom. He finally pulled the car out of the showroom and stood beside it. I looked at the car so seductively; I think I made him feel dirty. I ran my hand down the lines of the body. His mouth was agape.

I spun the keys around my finger. "Are you coming or not?" I asked.

He looked hesitant. "Yeah." He climbed in the passenger seat and started rubbing his thighs, like he was nervous.

I pulled out of the dealership and said, "You'd better buckle up." He frantically fastened his seat belt as I laid it down. I went about thirty miles over the speed limit.

"You need to slow down."

I laughed. "Am I making you nervous?" He said 'no' as he grabbed the door handle.

We went for a quick ride and then drove back to the dealership. I got out of the car and put the keys in my pocket. He slowly got out of the car, like he was hurt or something.

"Write it up, I'm driving it home. I trust you'll have someone drive my Mustang to my house for me."

"Yeah, yeah, anything you need."

I think he thought I was just messing with him. We went in his office and about thirty minutes later, after paperwork and my wire transfer, everyone in the dealership came by to make sure I had a good experience and I was happy with my purchase. The manager of the dealership even came by to tell me what a valued customer I was. He brought me a duffle bag filled with Audi goodies – a shirt, hat, stuffed animal, blanket, coffee mug and a key chain. You'd be surprised how nice everyone is when you pay in cash.

I pulled up to the diner and got out of my new toy. Bud and Carol came out.

"What is that?" she said, as she crossed her arms and walked around the car.

"This is the Audi R8 GT Spyder," I said, ignoring her tone.

"Oh my God," Bud cried. "I read about this in *Car & Driver* magazine. This is what, like, a hundred grand?" he asked enviously.

"Yeah, something like that," I said. "You want to drive it?" I threw him the keys.

He caught them in one hand. "Heck yeah, girl," he said as he got in the car.

"Megan, why would you buy a car like this?" Carol asked with her hands on her hips. "This is exactly the kind of thing your parents were worried about."

"Oh, lighten up, Carol." I said.

"Remember, money is the root of all evil." Bud said sarcastically, mocking Carol.

"Really?" I said. "I thought that was Wal-Mart."

"Megan," Carol said. "The *love* of money *is* the root of all evil."

"Good. I don't love the money, Carol, just the toys I can buy with it." Carol turned her back and went back into the diner.

Bud drove me around for a few minutes. He had a permanent smile on his face. He had never driven a car that handled like that before. He pulled up to the diner and I drove home. And I was alone again, even if I did have a cool new car.

★ ★ ★ ★ ★

Where was I going to park my new sweet ride? It looked like there was no better time to buy my oceanfront home. I called Jim Buchanan and he recommended a Realtor – Robert Costa. I gave Robert a list of what I wanted; oceanfront, with a dock, gym, gourmet kitchen, home theater, resort-style pool, tennis court, with security and it had to be at least two stories. Anything else was a bonus. It took him about three weeks to find the perfect house, but he did.

It was taupe, with bold white accents and black trim with palm trees all around it. The entrance had a circular driveway and displayed a water fountain within the circle where dolphins were spewing water – *classy*. The oversized front door was solid mahogany and was flanked by large marble pillars that presented a very old world feel. As soon as I stepped over the threshold, I knew I was home. As soon as you walked in, your eyes immediately fell on the topaz ocean just ahead. Even the smell was like home, it smelled like apple cider and cookies.

The inside of the house was filled with marble floors imported from Italy. There was a beautiful library to the left with a coffered ceiling. And, to the right was a sitting room. You could see the ocean from the kitchen, which was huge and evoked Tuscany, from the European cabinetry down to the natural stone.

Robert took me up the gray marble stairs, which had a wrought iron hand railing, even though there was an elevator. I gazed up at the enormous crystal chandelier above us. To the left was the master bedroom. It was huge. The bed was on a two-tiered platform and draped in fine silks, fit for a princess. The closet alone was bigger than any bedroom I had ever had. The master bathroom was encased in black marble and onyx. It was opulent and had another crystal chandelier hanging over a large tub.

It looked too large and lonely for a party of one. We walked back out into the bedroom and Robert opened the floor to ceiling drapes to reveal a large terrace overlooking the pool and ocean beyond. To the side of the house, was a nice canal flowing right into the Gulf. He showed me the other rooms upstairs. I hadn't even seen the rest of the house before I started deciding where the furniture would go. I made an offer and because it was all in cash, I moved right in.

The first time I stood on the balcony in my bedroom there was a purple evening sky. I had a beer in my hand and the palm trees swayed seductively in the breeze. As I studied the ocean merging with the night sky, I realized my life had become a postcard. At least – it looked like a postcard. I seemingly had everything, yet I was alone, right down to the empty guest house. How I wished things were different. How I hated being alone.

I finally found a home and it was in a neighborhood with other rich people. I was bound to find friendships or love here, right? I was in a perilous financial situation, socially. See, as it turns out, old money doesn't respect lottery money and neither do the 'nouveaux riche.' I am both the envy and enemy of most. So you tell me, where do I fit into society? Exactly: nowhere! I am in the same financial spectrum as these people, yet they make sure I cannot assimilate into their world. They all look down their noses, as if I don't deserve to even be in their presence.

I shouldn't say 'all' of them. Men are usually nice, but the women – they're not nice at all. They can't be nice to me out of fear I might want their husbands. It doesn't help I'm much younger than others with my net worth, or that I'm pretty. You know what else is not helpful? My title, 'The Lottery Heiress.' I could not pay for more press, and it is never good. And people believe *everything* they read about me. I'd hate me too, if I didn't know me!

CHAPTER 3

Henry Ford said, "Money doesn't change men, it merely unmasks them. If a man is naturally selfish or arrogant or greedy, the money brings that out, that's all." I've never been good with money. You know what you don't want to do to someone who's not good with money? You sure don't want to give them hundreds of millions of dollars.

It turned out I was a little selfish, arrogant and greedy. Wouldn't Henry Ford be disappointed in me – my parents would be pretty disappointed too. And the worst part was, the 'shopper's high' was always temporary. I bought clothes, cars, jewelry – and whatever else my little heart desired. Sometimes I bought things for other people, too. I didn't realize I was trying to fill a void inside of me. I knew I was unhappy.

People don't understand. They think money can solve all your problems and make you happy. That is such crap. The biggest one being no one leaves me alone. Everyone wants money; I've had to hire a full-time security team because people have attacked me, stalked me and tried to date me or befriend me just to get money. I got to a point where I didn't want to leave the house.

It's a very lonely life. I substituted material things for companionship.

On one of my shopping sprees, I remember being told how much my purchase was and handing over my credit card without even listening. And it hit me… no budget, no counting and no more keeping track of my spending. I bought whatever I wanted, without once looking at a price tag. My spending got out of control very quickly. But it didn't matter. I had so much money it just didn't matter.

Carol stepped in as my advisor and make-shift mother. In fact, she held a financial intervention of sorts. She gathered my attorney and a few other people at the newly-renovated diner and they made me promise to take a Dave Ramsey course so I could learn how to manage my money better. I did it just to get them off my back, but I was annoyed by it. Who were they kidding? I could have flown Dave Ramsey himself in to teach me if I wanted to.

I was also getting in trouble with my car collection. I made the mistake of going to the Sebring Raceway to watch the famous annual event, the *12 Hours of Sebring*. They race Corvettes and Audis and Porsches, oh my. I wanted every car I saw on the racetrack, and I bought several of them.

It wasn't being raced, but I met a guy in the parking lot driving a Bugatti. He let me take it for a spin. It had a 1,200 horsepower, 16-cylinder engine. He told me it went from 0 – 60 in 2.6 seconds. He was right! I had never felt so close to a car. I could almost hear the engine whispering 'I love you' every time I turned the corners. The leather interior held me so snugly, I felt like I was being cradled in a giant's hand. I had to have one.

People always make derogatory comments about people driving expensive cars – like they're trying to over-compensate for something. Well, speaking on behalf of all millionaires, we just like nice cars!

I was not about to wait the year or more of production time to build and customize my Bugatti, so I contacted the headquarters in France and they helped me acquire a pre-owned model to my taste. It took several months, and I grew very impatient. But Bugatti finally called and said my car was on its way. I asked them to drop it off in front of the diner so I could show everyone. Not everyone was as excited as I was.

Of course, Bud was, because he loved cars as much as I did. But I seriously thought Carol was going to have a heart attack. She made it crystal clear she disapproved of me spending a million dollars on one car. Her voice was getting so high when she was scolding me, the neighborhood dogs came to bark at the diner doors and windows. She was very upset. I had to remind her that she wasn't my mother and that it was *my* money.

The car carrier pulled up and Bud and I ran outside. Carol came out and crossed her arms and shook her head disapprovingly.

I looked at her. "That's it, Carol, you just lost the first ride. You coming, Bud?"

"You're kidding, right?" He was so excited, like a little kid. A crowd from the pier started gathering around the car and asking questions. Most people have never seen a car like this, and then having it dropped off at the most visible spot at the beach – well, it was quite a spectacle.

The driver backed it off the carrier. It was black and it was streamlined like a jet. It was like a cross between the

Batmobile from the old Adam West show and a car from the future. It looked like a prototype. It looked like it could fly! And it would, with me behind the wheel. I signed the paperwork and ripped the keys from the driver's hand.

Bud and I got in and I drove all the way to Naples. We went straight to 5th Ave. and parked in front of a restaurant where we ate outside, just so we could watch everyone look at the car. The waiter told me he loved my car and started flirting with me, after I explained Bud wasn't my sugar daddy. I wound up leaving him a huge tip.

Everyone at the restaurant who saw us pull up was complimenting Bud. I thought it was funny that they assumed it was his. We overheard a woman say he must be having a mid-life crisis and we laughed. I enjoyed every minute of that meal, until we were getting back into the car. That was when a reporter from a local newspaper, Joseph Carr, slithered up behind me and I didn't know it.

While we were sitting on the patio, I'd noticed someone putting flyers on everyone's car windshield along 5th Ave. I wanted to get back to the Bugatti before this clown touched it. But I didn't make it. He slapped a paper on my windshield and plunked the wiper over it, causing the alarm to blare and say in a robotic voice, "Back away from the vehicle. You are too close to vehicle." Bud knew I was angry. The guy saw me as I walked up to him.

"Jesus loves you," he said with an apprehensive smile.

I grabbed the paper and crumpled it and threw it at the saint. "I know he does. But, he *hates* litter. Pick that up. How many trees are you going to kill trying to save my soul?" He picked up the paper I threw at him, looking very upset and walked away quickly. Bud just shook his head at me. Unfortunately, Joseph witnessed the whole thing.

Joseph stepped up to me as I was opening the door. "That poor guy just wanted to save you from eternal damnation," he said, oh so sincere.

"What are *you* doing here?" I asked.

"I heard someone was showing off their Bugatti and I just had a feeling it was you. There are a lot of kids going to bed without dinner tonight; I hope you think about that on the way home."

"What's your problem, man?" Bud said across the car.

"Jealous much?" I asked.

"No, I'm not jealous. I'm just wondering what you're doing to help poor people today, Heiress." I was the same height as Joseph but today I had four inch heels on. I was glad to make him look small.

"Why don't you pick on someone your own size, Mr. Carr? Just follow the yellow brick road." Bud laughed. I got in the car. Joseph leaned on the car so I couldn't move.

"Get off my car, now," I yelled as I changed from heels to my driving moccasins.

"I'm really hungry," Joseph whined. "Why don't you buy me lunch and I won't write about you and your new car?"

I laughed. "You think you can extort lunch from me?" I said as I got into the seat.

Bud yelled over the car, "Megan, do you want me to…?" but I shook my head.

Joseph went on a tirade, looking around to see how big a scene he could create. "What about the poor people in this area, Heiress? Why do you hate poor people so much?" he yelled.

I stood up as much as I could in the car and yelled back. "I love poor people, now get off my Bugatti!"

He didn't, so I peeled out, and he rolled off the fender and landed on the sidewalk. Bud looked at me. "I can't wait to see tomorrow's headline." I knew he was right, but I didn't exactly have a choice.

We drove back toward home and Bud didn't say anything for a long time. He finally spoke up about half way back. "You were hard on that guy, Megan."

"Stop! Not you, too?"

"It's fun having all this money sometimes, but it's not making you very happy, is it?"

"Happiness is overrated," I said.

"I disagree," he said. "In fact, I pray for your happiness every night."

I rolled my eyes. "You don't know what it's like to be me, okay? You have no idea."

"Look, you just seem like you're more and more miserable as time goes on." he said.

"Really? And you're happy Bud? At least I'm not in love with someone and denying it."

I was referring to Carol. It was no secret he was beyond smitten and wouldn't tell her.

"I think we should stop talking," he said.

"That's the best idea you've had today."

The next day, Bud and I opened the paper at the diner. The headline read, "The Lottery Heiress Buys Million Dollar Car While Neighbors Starve."

"You're going to get in a lot of trouble with this car, Megan." Bud said.

"And this headline is ridiculous. No one in *my*

neighborhood is starving," I said as I threw the paper down.

"You make yourself an easy target, Meg."

"I know," I said. I just hated the fact Carr was right. I shouldn't have bought it.

"You're going to have to step up security because of this article," he said.

"Why is it so easy for everyone to hate me?" I asked.

Everyone answered, "The money!"

I looked around at them all, knowing they were right. Then Eddy came up to me. "I've always liked you, Megan. I don't care about the money," he said.

"Thanks, Eddy. I wish everyone had your heart," I said. I didn't understand why someone wanted to write stories about me when there were real problems in the world.

Everywhere I went for the next few weeks, people protested my million dollar car. They shouted rude things, held up handwritten signs, and actually threw stuff at me and my car. I couldn't believe all the negative attention I was getting for driving Boo – that's what I named him. I decided it was time to go to the source of the problem.

I called Mr. Carr to find out what his motives were for trying to destroy me. His assistant kept taking messages, but I assumed he was just refusing to take my phone calls. So I got in my pick-up truck and drove down to the newspaper office to confront him in person. The receptionist acted like she didn't know who I was. But when I said, "I'm The Lottery Heiress," her eyes got as big as saucers.

I guess she really didn't know who Megan Pagano was. How sad. My name was just a name on a bank account, but everyone knew who 'The Lottery Heiress' was. She apologized and told me Joseph wasn't available. I gave her a dirty look and walked out the door without saying anything.

I had a plan. I would just wait in the parking lot for him. All weasels pop out of their holes to eat eventually. It was only about thirty minutes before he showed up.

I opened the door to my truck and he saw me. He rolled his eyes at me. "What are you doing here?" he asked.

"Why do you think I'm here?" I snapped. "You don't even know me. What gives you the right to print outright lies about me?"

He looked down, "Look, I'm just trying to make a name for myself here."

"Oh, you didn't need to do that. I already *have* a name for you, *Jackass.*" Surprisingly, he laughed. And I drove away.

I spent the next month giving millions of dollars away. I hired a public relations firm to cover all the good deeds I did. I had a medical clinic built in a bad part of town, I donated an eighteen wheeler full of food for victims of a recent tornado, and I bought poor children clothes and shoes. I directed my public relations team to 'leak' my good deeds to the local news. After all, even doctors need doctors, and I wasn't going to convince anyone by doing my own publicity.

It worked for a few weeks, but people got sick of seeing my face, and Joseph still wrote nasty articles about me – mostly about me doing charity work just for the publicity. The sad part was, he was kind of right this time. And in spite of all the good I did, I swear people saw me as a huge dollar sign instead of a person. I am so tired of people asking me, "Could you write a check to blah, blah, blah?"

I don't even like going anywhere because everyone wants something and I *hate* that part of having money. No matter what I give or how many hours I volunteer, it's never enough. People write articles about me or post rude comments on the internet about how I *waste* money. I do waste money, but I also give millions away. And besides, it's mine to waste!

It's all about public perception. No one wants to read the good things, but if I get a ticket for speeding, or have too many drinks, or spend a hundred grand on a car, there it is in the paper. Mr. Carr has it in for me. What did I ever do to him? And the sad part was, he was actually a good writer. I sometimes read his articles, even when I wasn't the subject.

Unfortunately, my driving habits did catch up with me. I was warned, and I didn't take it seriously. The last ticket I got really hurt. I had to go to court again, my fourth time in a year.

And of course, I got a total misogynist in court. The judge looked at my attorney, then at me. "Young lady, you have been in my courtroom before, haven't you?"

"Yes, your honor," I said.

He looked at the ticket, and apparently noticed I was driving my Bugatti this time. "Did you crash your Porsche?"

My attorney, Aaron Davis, stepped in, "Your honor, my client has more than one car. She has never been in an accident."

"Well, Mr. Davis that is a miracle in itself. Your client is going to kill someone – probably some innocent bystander." He looked right at me and took his glasses off. "I thought you told me last time I would never see you in my courtroom again. So, tell me, why are you here again for the same offense?"

"What can I say, your honor? I *missed* you." The courtroom laughed. My attorney shook his head. The judge banged his gavel.

"Well, you're really going to miss me now. I am revoking your driving privileges for a year. That's all I can do under the law. Smarten up before you kill someone. Pay your fines at...you know the routine." He looked at me sternly. "Ms. Pagano, I hope I *never* see you again."

It wasn't the first time a man said that to me. I was sure it wouldn't be the last. Meanwhile, I had to hire a driver if I wanted to go anywhere. I was not going to be chauffeured around in some ridiculous limo, so I bought a Range Rover. I hired a driver through the security company I used. I always had security – most people couldn't tell because they blended into the crowd. I was constantly surrounded, and if they weren't in my car, they were in the car behind me.

I interviewed a few different people. One stuck out in the mix. Although they all had similar military backgrounds, two of them were cute and single. Even I knew that wasn't a good idea. I hired the married one. His name was James. He was also from New England.

He was in his mid-forties, and had two children. He kept my attitude in check. He made snarky comments to me, but he did it with humor, and I appreciated his candor. When you're as rich as I am, no one has the coconuts to speak the truth to you. I did miss driving my fast cars around, but I never had to find a parking space myself. That was nice.

One of the first things he made me do was bulletproof my vehicles. He found out about the security problems I'd had in the past and thought this was a good way to prevent something serious from happening. I know it seems crazy to have a convertible and spend all the money to bulletproof my other vehicles.

The simple explanation is, I always thought I could outrun a bullet in any of my cars. I know, it's *stupid*, but in my head, I thought it was possible. It took a couple of weeks to customize my Range Rover. When I went with James to pick it up, I wanted to test it to make sure it was indeed bulletproof. I didn't think this was an unreasonable request. I was, after all, paying for a bulletproof vehicle.

When James and I got to the shop, we were met by the owner, Mr. Rodriguez. He was well known in Naples and had many celebrities as clients. He came over to shake my hand.

"How are you, Ms. Pagano? I'm glad to see you. I think our work will please you."

"I can't wait to see it."

"It's right over here," he said. He walked us over to the Range Rover. It didn't look any different, except for the rims and tires, and window tint.

"You stand behind your work, Mr. Rodriguez?" I asked.

"Yes, ma'am. As you know, we have many celebrity clients."

I inspected the Range Rover. Without turning my head, I asked, "What are you carrying today, James?"

He responded hesitantly, "My Glock."

I put my hand out. "May I?" James reluctantly placed the gun in my hand.

This made Mr. Rodriguez very nervous. "What are you going to do?"

I turned and stared at him. "Shoot my car," I said. What a stupid question!

James said to Mr. Rodriguez, "You're going to want to back up." Mr. Rodriguez backed way, way up.

James moved closer to me. I held the gun up and pointed it at the car and I called back to Mr. Rodriguez, "I hope your work is as good as you say it is."

"You might want to cover your ears," James yelled to him.

I fired the first shot into the front window and it bounced off, taking just a tiny chip with it. I shot the back passenger side door and it ricocheted, with the same result. Finally, I shot the rear tire and the bullet just dropped to the ground.

I handed the gun back to James. "Thanks," I said.

Mr. Rodriguez crept back in our direction. "Well, Mr. Rodriguez, I am very impressed," I said. He just looked at me like I was crazy. "I would like you to fix that little mess..." I gestured to the little nicks I'd put in the car, "...and then have it delivered. I will be sending the rest of my cars in as well."

Mr. Rodriguez was apprehensive, "Thank you?" Apparently, people don't shoot at their cars. Like I'm going to take someone at their word!

One afternoon, James drove me to Naples so I could go

to Cartier. I had a gala to attend, and I wanted some new jewelry. I spent half a million dollars on jewelry in about half an hour – it's not difficult to do in Cartier. The salesman was named Brent. He was very good looking and as he was wrapping up my jewelry, he asked me if I wanted anything else.

I stared at him. "Are you married?"

He looked at me with a mischievous smile. "No, I'm not."

"Do you have a girlfriend?"

He pulled out his phone and I watched him text, *It's over. Sorry.* He said, "Not anymore."

I grinned. "What time do you get off?"

He looked at his watch and said, "Right now." He told one of his co-workers he was leaving and we walked out the door.

We got outside and James asked me if I needed help with my packages. I said, "No, James."

"Good, he looks heavy," he said sarcastically as he opened the back door. "Where do you want to go?"

"How about dinner?" Brent suggested.

"Sounds good," I said. Shopping is so draining! We drove around for a little bit and got to know each other. Then I had James take us to one of the most exclusive restaurants in town.

The guy was gorgeous, but lacking any real substance. Lucky for me, I wasn't seeking any. I tried to talk about politics and he said he didn't really pay attention to that kind of 'stuff.' 'Stuff?' I thought. How can anyone not care about politics? Anyway, over the course of dinner, I tried to find out what we had in common. There was nothing! Oh well, we're both attractive. It was enough for the moment. It wasn't like I wanted to get married.

About the time dessert came, he mentioned my neck was turning red. Then I noticed my arms, then my hands. The next morning, I went to an allergist where a rich person's worst nightmare comes true. No, not kidnapping, extortion or blackmail. An allergy to gold! How cruel, indeed. I had never heard of anyone being allergic to gold.

I had worn gold all of my life. The doctor told me sometimes people just develop an allergy to gold with no warning. He said only nine percent of the world's population is allergic to gold. Why me? How embarrassing, to physically break out from excessive spending. Needless to say, I never saw him again.

I got my license back a year later. I kept James on as my bodyguard. We formed a great friendship. He would accompany me on shopping trips or dates. He was there in case I ran into trouble, and I made enough of my own without outside help. I did plenty of newsworthy things in the following year. I drank way too much. I bought more cars. And I posted evidence of my stupidity on this new thing called "Facebook."

Although I decided to make the beach house my permanent home, I retreated to the river house when I needed a break from the beach, which was only about a weekend a month.

My neighbor at the river house was a commercial pilot. One day, I was staring out the back lanai facing the river and I heard this noise. I stepped outside to investigate. I saw a little seaplane, and a few minutes later my neighbor landed it in front of our docks. I charged down to the dock and asked him to take me up in it. It was both terrifying and exhilarating. By the time we landed, I had decided to get my pilot's license and – you guessed it – a plane.

I was tired of wasting my time on gorgeous, empty men. I was getting bored. I was living the American dream, right? I mean, I had people catering to my every need. I had everything I could ever want at the point of my finger. Isn't that what we all dream of at one point or another? But I still wasn't happy and I didn't know why.

I disagree with Henry Ford. Money does change you. Sometimes it makes you do stupid things. Like, when you forget you're richer than most of the people on the planet and you can't do things you once considered normal. For example: I love thrift stores. I used to buy a lot of clothes from thrift stores. It's not weird, most of the millionaires I know shop at thrift stores. I just made the mistake of not thinking through the details.

On one particular day, I went to a thrift store by myself. I get in trouble when I talk to people outside of my inner circle, people who don't know me. I made small talk with a few people in the store. They were saying how the economy had been so bad they've had to sacrifice on small things, such as not ordering a pizza or buying a new outfit for a whole year! I dug down deep and channeled my inner blue-collar, middle-class self and said some sympathetic things. Unfortunately, when they came out of the store, they saw me getting into my Lamborghini. They didn't say anything, but they looked truly disgusted.

I offered to buy them a pizza, at which one of them responded by flipping up their middle finger and saying, "Watch the birdie."

I yelled back, "Hey, that's not a real bird." Should you ever get the opportunity, DO NOT drive a Lamborghini to a thrift store. Of course, that little escapade made the newspaper. I don't remember the exact title but it wasn't a proud moment.

★ ★ ★ ★ ★

Weeks later, I put an old record on, propped my feet up on the coffee table and starting drinking. I went through a six-pack – quickly. The phone rang. It was the security guard at my gate asking if Phillip Mason could come through. I said he could. A minute later, I saw Phillip hop out of the passenger side of a car and head to my door. Annoyed at the interruption to my pity party, I opened the door.

Now, at this point in the story, it had been about a year and two months since I had seen him. He looked different. His posture and gait had changed and he looked like he'd gained fifteen pounds. He was even a little grayer, a little paler. This is Florida – it wouldn't kill him to catch some rays.

"Hello," he said, then pushed my door open and walked inside, taking a look around at how I was living now.

"Hi, former life," I said. He looked at all the empty beer bottles lying around. I definitely had a little buzz, and I spoke real carefully so he wouldn't hear me slur my words.

"Drinking alone, huh? That's not good," he said.

"Well, it helps me forget I'm an orphan and have a jerky ex-fiancé to remember."

"Look, Megan, I may have been a little premature in breaking off our engagement."

I laughed at him. "Oh, well, it wouldn't be the first thing you've been premature about."

He sat down and put his head in his hands. "I'm in

trouble, Megan."

I put my hands in the air, "Well, you know it can't be mine." I laughed again.

"Megan, this is serious," he said.

"Save your breath, Phillip. I know about Julian embezzling money from you. I always thought he was up to something. What I don't understand is what you're doing *here*."

"I signed over Power of Attorney to Julian when I went to Germany with one of my clients and that's when he… you know. My attorneys think I'm in real trouble. It wasn't just my money, there were investors." He followed me into the kitchen and kept talking. I opened the fridge and grabbed another beer. He looked at me with his mopey face, seeking compassion.

"Beer?" I asked.

"No. Look, I know you're the last person I should be coming to for help but I need a few million dollars just so I can float payroll and my mortgages. I hate to ask…" he said, looking down at the floor. I popped the top off my beer and took a swig, wondering which one of us was more pathetic.

"Ugh, I'll go get my checkbook," I said. Was it just the beer, or the memory of him that motivated me to write him a check?

"I can't thank you enough for this," he said as he waved the check at me. "Well, I have to go. I need to get back to Miami." He rushed out the door and I noticed Melinda Brennan, office piranha, waiting in the car outside my front door, with the motor running. I had always despised her and the feeling was mutual.

"Is that Melinda?" I asked.

"Yeah, she came with me for the ride."

I looked at my watch and pretended to be concerned. "Gosh, I hope she doesn't miss her Weight Watchers meeting!"

"She didn't want me to be alone," he snapped.

"I'm sure!" I snapped back.

"Megan, I know you and Melinda have had your differences."

"Yeah, call me crazy, I didn't like people hitting on my fiancé. Wow, I am such a jerk. And now I get to cover her paychecks. Yippee."

He stopped and held the car door. "Megan, whether you believe it or not, I still love you." He actually looked sincere.

"I know. That's why I haven't heard from you in over a year, right?"

"You're the best, Megan," he said as he kissed my cheek.

"I know. Good luck, Phillip." I slammed the house door thinking it would be the last time I would ever see Phillip. Through the window, I watched him get in the car. He looked at the check and shook his head. I hoped he was enjoying the memo line, which read 'Viagra.'

I sat down on the sofa and started thinking about Phillip. I likened him to a hot cup of coffee on a cold day. It looks so nice and frothy. Your hands are cold; you think to yourself this coffee will warm up your tummy and your hands at the same time – what a great thing to have in your possession.

Then, after fifteen minutes, you're almost finished with that cup of coffee and you find something really disgusting sitting at the bottom. I mean, it's clear it's not coffee grounds, but you can't really identify it. And you think, "I should've just had water, at least I could have seen through it."

★ ★ ★ ★ ★

Months passed and I woke up one day to read an article Joseph Carr had written about his daughter, Liz. She was dying from a disease with a lot of letters that I'd never heard of. He begged people in the community to go to the hospital to see if they were a donor match.

She needed several transfusions but even if she got them, they weren't sure she would make it. Anyway, someone rumored to be wealthy was a match and saved that little girl's life anonymously. People speculated it was me, but I vehemently denied it. Anyone who knows me knows I hate needles and I hate to say it – I hated her father.

I was still getting into lots of trouble and Carol was concerned. She suggested that I start actually helping at the diner. So, I occasionally popped in to make biscuits and make up stupid names for the daily specials. It was right around the time we hired a new waitress at Big Mama's. Her name was Jennifer.

She was a recovering addict living in a halfway house. Normally, I wouldn't have hired someone like that. But she had kids and it bothered me that she was trying to get them back and no one would give her a job. I believe in second chances.

She worked for me about a year before I let her move in to my guest house at the beach. I thought she had kicked the drugs. She was extremely reliable at work. She didn't come in late once the whole year. But it turned out she was seeing her ex-boyfriend again and had fallen back into the drug scene. The worst part was she knew I kept a lot of cash in my safe at the beach house.

One day while I was in the kitchen of my beach house, she and her boyfriend attacked me. They promised if I gave them all the cash in the safe, they wouldn't hurt me. So I did, and they beat me anyway – until I was unconscious. I had no security team because I was in my own stupid house, and there was no panic button under the counter where they had cornered me. How convenient.

Carol found me because I didn't show up to meet her for lunch. She said I was laying on the floor next to a frying pan with blood and hair on it. I was in a coma for days. They didn't know if I was going to have brain damage or if I was going to even come out of the coma. The doctor told Carol and Bud it was touch-and-go, but he and his staff were doing everything they could.

Meanwhile, I was someplace other than the hospital room. I was walking on a beach somewhere. I looked at the waves on the right. There was no one on the beach except me. Then, I looked to my left and a man with long hair and a beard was standing there.

"Jesus?" I asked.

"Hello, Megan." He smiled.

"Am I in heaven?" I asked.

"No, Megan. You're in a coma. You were beaten unconscious by someone you gave a second chance to. While you're here, we'll talk about second chances. Let's walk." So, we started walking. "I want you to understand that your life is not your own. You need to start making better choices. There are many lessons you have yet to learn. And you don't have much time."

"Am I going to die?" I asked.

"No, I'm sending you back. But please remember you belong to me. I know you want love. But you need to understand sex is different from love. Sex is a gift, but you need to be married first. And money hasn't brought you much happiness, has it? Remember, the love of money is the root of all evil."

"I do good things with the money."

"Megan, you need to focus on the reason you're here with me," he said. Suddenly, off to my right there was a hot guy with long dark hair and a rock hard body in a small loin cloth coming out of the surf. He smiled at me and waved slowly for me to come into the water. I turned and started walking towards him.

Jesus said, "You get distracted easily." Jesus waved his hand and the other guy vanished. "Oh, that David. He's still got it." Where did that hot guy go? And who was David?

Jesus kept on talking. "I will send you a husband. I have picked someone out for you. It's not someone you will expect. I will give you the signs. Pay attention. Until then, be faithful to me. Remember, I am with you always." And then he vanished too.

I woke up with a loud exhale in my hospital bed. Carol was standing there.

"Megan?"

"Hey Carol. What's new?" I said.

"What's new?" She started to laugh, crying at the same time. "Well, I learned the whole hospital thinks your biscuits are the best in town."

"Did they see them during my sponge bath?"

She laughed. "She's back! Do you know what happened?"

"Yeah, I was in a coma for three days."

Carol looked at me, puzzled. "Megan, how could you have known that?"

"Jesus told me," I said. She looked at Bud in disbelief.

Bud asked, "What kind of dope are they giving her? You scared us, kid." He said, "I'm glad you're back. They didn't know if you would...." His voice cracked with emotion. "Well, never mind, you're okay, now."

"Carol. Jesus said he's sending me a husband," I said.

"Wow. That's great, honey." She said as she grabbed my hand.

I touched my face. "My face hurts. Am I ugly now?" I wasn't sure I wanted to know the answer.

Bud laughed. "No uglier than you've ever been."

Carol said, "You're going to be fine. You didn't need stitches on your face, and they said you'll have a scar on your head, but your hair will grow over it."

I touched my head. "Oh, I'm bald."

"Sorry, Megan. They had to shave your head. They had to put stitches on your scalp," she said. Carol told me later on that God used dreams in the Bible and we shouldn't be so quick to dismiss a dream like the one I had. I think secretly she was hoping it was my wake up call.

For weeks, I lay in my hospital bed, thinking about my life. There are only so many empty things you can have before they take a toll on you. Empty homes, empty cars, empty holidays, empty relationships, empty beer cans. Sometimes they mingled in various combinations.

I'm not going to lie, I liked going anywhere I wanted, having any man I wanted, doing anything I wanted. But I was constantly wondering why I was still so empty inside. I had everything the world says I should have to make me happy. Why was I so unhappy and dissatisfied? It didn't make any sense to me. I told Carol I would go to church with her as soon as I made it out of the hospital.

Joseph Carr didn't ease up on me even after the coma. He wondered if I provoked the attack. Unbelievable! That should prove to people I wasn't his daughter's blood donor.

A court date was set up for Jennifer and her boyfriend, who pleaded no contest. Instead of jail time, they were both sentenced to a rehab program – which I was not happy about. More than my injuries, I wanted them to pay for what they did to my *hair*. But, I guess as long as they got clean, that was all that mattered. I didn't want them to do that to anyone else.

Once I was released from the hospital, I kept putting off going to church with Carol. I guess I did what people do right before a diet – they binge on everything in sight. I wasn't ready to give up on men and beer – who knew when I'd get more? I'd never gone in for the whole religious thing. I wasn't ready to quit cold turkey. And yet, it's not like I could totally go back to my old life style, with that Jesus vision or whatever it was constantly haunting me.

★ ★ ★ ★ ★

A few weeks after the coma, at Carol's constant nagging, I was ready to go to church. It wasn't a pretty church. It was very plain in the inside. There weren't even any windows in the sanctuary. I found out why later on – it was built to withstand a Category 5 hurricane.

I was supposed to meet Carol inside, but I didn't see her anywhere. I heard the music start, and even someone like me doesn't want to be late for church. Since I didn't get struck down by lightning just walking in, I found a seat next to two older ladies. They leered at me and then looked at each other, like I was the last person on earth that would go to church. I looked around the room. Where the heck was Carol? She had told me she would be there early, so we could sit together.

I was very uncomfortable. I felt like everyone was staring at me. Well, actually, they were. I was wearing designer clothes, make-up and driving a very expensive car. It looked like the people here didn't have much money, or maybe they didn't care about money. I used to be like that too. They only knew what they read about me, and I bet they believed it all. They were probably wondering what the rotten 'Lottery Heiress' was even doing there.

Finally, Carol came over and sat down.

"Where were you?" I asked.

"Sorry, I was talking with someone out in the hall," she said apologetically. She noticed I kept looking around. "What are you looking at?"

"I'm wondering what kind of whack jobs are in here," I said. She started to laugh.

"I think we can safely assume everyone is here is trying to be a better person!" She couldn't stop chuckling, even when the choir stood up and started singing.

"Did I ever tell you, when I was in college, I had a married professor who used to hit on me all the time?"

"I've heard of married professors hitting on their students before!"

"Not ones who are deacons in their church."

"Megan, most of the people who claim they're Christians don't even read the Bible."

"It's pretty bad when I'm not any worse than people who go to church!"

A loud 'Shhhh!' came from a little old lady behind us.

Carol turned around and introduced us. "Betty, this is my friend, Megan I told you about." The woman just nodded and didn't put her hand out.

I turned around and introduced myself, "Megan *Pagan*, how's it going?" I asked with a nod.

"Hi." She said with a half-hearted smile.

Carol looked at me with a smile and shook her head at my sudden name change.

"Maybe it's just me, but I feel like I have a real connection with that lady," I said sarcastically. Carol just smiled and shook her head.

The preacher talked about how the things of this world can't make us happy. People shouted stuff out during the sermon. "Amen," "Hallelujah," "Preach on." Clearly these people didn't grow up in a Catholic Church like I did, where the only acceptable noise during service is snoring.

How long would it be before someone came up to me asking for money? It happens all the time. That's why you hear about millionaires building bowling alleys and movie theaters in their homes. We don't like being harassed by people. I didn't grow up with money. That's why I went to college and had a career, so I wouldn't have to ask people for money.

Anyway, the preacher went on about how we can leave our sins behind and how God can give us a clean slate. That sounded pretty good to me. I'd lived the last five years of my life in excess, and I'd enjoyed most of it. Carol said there's a passage in the Bible that says sin is fun for a season.

The problem is this is Florida, there's really no change of season down here. It's very confusing for sinners. But I was at the point where I was ready for a change. I could quit the beer and the boyfriends for a while, right? The preacher claimed my life wasn't about me at all. Was it true?

Then he asked if we were ready to face God on Judgment Day. I hated the thought of measuring my life by the Ten Commandments – I broke a few every day.

He said if there was no God, then it didn't matter how we lived our lives. But he said if he was right, we will be judged according to the way we live. He said according to Jesus, if I even looked at a man with lust, I had committed adultery with him in my heart. If that's the case, I'm *really* in trouble.

The preacher went on to say Jesus died to take the penalty for our sins, because we couldn't be perfect, but Jesus was. Well, I didn't know much about perfection, but Lord knows I was good at sinning.

Finally the pastor asked if anyone in the congregation needed to repent and accept Jesus as their savior. I remembered my vision in the hospital and found myself walking down the aisle. I heard one of the old ladies behind me say, "Did someone tell her the pastor baptizes new believers in beer?" Then they started snickering. I guess my reputation preceded me.

I didn't care. I was ready for a change and I knew this would be a change. If Jesus couldn't help me control my appetite for men, beer and expensive toys, I knew nothing could.

The room was filled with gasps and whispers when I got to the front of the church. It wasn't exactly the reception I was expecting from a room filled with dirty, rotten sinners. I wanted to find out what kind of weird tenets the church had, so after the service, I asked Carol to introduce me to the pastor.

"Oh, 'The Lottery Heiress,'" he said.

"Please call me Megan. Most of the things written about me aren't true," I said.

"Well, I'm glad to hear that!"

"Pastor, I do have some questions though," I said.

"Sure," he said joyfully. "I'm happy to answer them."

"Pastor, do you think it's a sin for women to wear pants?" I asked.

"Of course not!" he said.

"Do you think it's a sin for women to dye their hair?" I asked.

"No, it's not!" he said with a smile.

"Do you think it's a sin if women wear make-up?" I asked.

"I tell you the truth," he said with a smile, "it's a sin when some women don't!" The three of us laughed. I decided I'd be okay at this church.

The next week I took a class about what it meant to be a church member and I decided to get baptized, right away. The congregation clapped when I got baptized but I think some of them were waiting to see if I made a sizzling noise as I entered the baptismal. Sorry, no sizzle sinners!

I spoke with the pastor and asked him what I could do financially to help the church. I asked what his operating budget was and I asked him if the church had a Benevolence Fund. He said of course they did. I asked him if five million dollars was enough to add to it for now. He almost choked as he said yes.

Then I asked him how much the mortgage payoff was. He said it was just under five million dollars. So I told him I would write a check for ten million dollars. That way they could start putting funds toward mission trips, which he said was their primary concern. He started to tear up.

"Please, no crying," I said. "I can't take it."

"I'm sorry," he said, "I have just been praying for this money and having you here to deliver it is a miracle."

"Well, if the miracle is me being in church and still being alive, yes, I guess it is a miracle."

He shook the check. "You don't know how much good we are going to do with this money. Thank you," he said as he hugged me. I just stood there, but he didn't let go, so I patted his back awkwardly.

I asked him to follow me out to the parking lot. I walked him over to my beloved Bugatti. "This car has just been sitting in my garage. It has brought nothing but trouble." I placed the keys in his hand. "The title's in the glove box." He gazed at the keys in disbelief. "I can also find a buyer, so you can get the most money," I said.

He grinned wildly at me. "That would be great. We are so glad to have you become part of our church."

"Thank you," I said. As Carol and I got into her car, we saw the pastor and his wife peel out of the parking lot in the Bugatti. What a hoot!

CHAPTER 4

At the good pastor's recommendation, I joined the singles group, led by a pastor named Andy. He seemed like a nice guy. His wife, Jill, seemed okay but she wasn't very outgoing, so it made her hard to read. The class was on Friday nights, which was good. Being new to this whole church thing, I thought this would be a good place to ask questions. I was wrong.

Andy was talking about sin. I didn't really grasp what he was saying. So I asked him to explain it. He said I shouldn't do anything God says is a sin, but I should also avoid doing anything that would cause other people to sin. Now I was really confused.

He said, "You shouldn't drink if it would cause an unbeliever to get drunk or cheat or commit any other sins." Then he said, "I know how women like to buy shoes, but they shouldn't buy an excessive amount of shoes. And ladies, if shopping too much makes someone else shop too much, then you are causing someone else to sin." So I asked him if that was subjective – the amount of excess?

Then, he told the guys not to look at women with lust

because it was a sin.

"Andy, you don't think women struggle with lust?" I asked.

"No, I don't think most women struggle with lust, Megan. I believe women struggle with shopping and being good stewards of money," he said, confidently.

"Well, I think about men all the time," I said.

Andy and the women in the group were not pleased with my candor. However, I noticed the guys in my group were very attentive. They were actually pretty interested in what I had to say.

"I mean, I can't have sex now until I get married, right?" I asked.

"Right, you need to wait until you're married," he said looking around the room. "Let's move on, everyone." What he meant was, 'Stop talking, Megan.' I asked how I could just quit having sex, cold turkey, after having sex my whole adult life. Andy was visibly uncomfortable.

His face was red. He tried to loosen his necktie, but he wasn't wearing one. I just wanted to know how I was going to stop doing something I enjoyed. I told him I could give up the beer, and even cussing, but sex? That was going to be difficult. He kept saying I would need to make an appointment to talk with him more in depth.

Then I asked if praying to Jesus every day would help suppress my sinful desires. I thought he'd have an easy answer to that one. But again, there he was with the red face. He seemed like he would have been happier if I'd never shown up. Maybe if I had never joined the church.

"I have to wait for marriage to have sex? That's like buying a car without test driving it," I said. "It's ridiculous." The guys snickered. The women all sat with their arms folded across their chests.

Andy said, "It is good to remain single, that way you can focus on God and his plan."

"But the Apostle Paul said if we can't control ourselves, we should marry because it's better to marry than burn with passion."

He cleared his throat. "Right, but marriage shouldn't be your first priority, okay? That's all I'm saying."

"Well, I don't know about anyone else, but I burn with passion. I need to get married – *quickly*." I noticed a guy smirking with his arms folded. He was thoroughly amused by the exchange between me and Andy. His name tag said 'Rick.'

Andy was getting extremely irritated by my questions. "Look, you should only get married if you can't control yourself. Haven't you got any self-control?" he asked, running his fingers aggressively through his hair.

I said, "I couldn't help notice that *you're* married." The guys in the group started laughing. Andy's wife looked terrified. No doubt she was anxious about Andy's reaction – which, I don't have to tell you, wasn't good. Andy had so many veins pop out of his forehead and neck, he looked like a Klingon.

I was concerned about him myself, and I decided it was time to leave. I thought about telling him to go to Walgreens on the way home, it looked like he needed that little arm thingy in front of the pharmacy that measures your blood pressure. But I decided he would probably just want me to pray for him – which I did.

I stood up. "I think I'm just going to join the women's Bible study on Tuesdays," I announced. "I'm sorry everyone, I don't think I will be returning."

Andy gasped with relief and said, "Thank you. And Megan, you can come by my office anytime, as long as you agree to leave the door open." I just laughed, hard, and said goodbye to the group. One of the guys from the group followed me out to my car. It was Rick.

"Megan?"

"What are you doing following me out to my car?"

"I'm a new Christian too. I am struggling with all this too. Have you eaten dinner yet?"

"Wow. This is pretty brazen of you to ask me to dinner after hearing all that." He just shrugged his shoulders. "Do you know who I am?" I asked.

"Nope. I just moved down from Connecticut."

"What do you do?"

"I'm a firefighter."

"And you don't know who I am?"

"No, but I think we have a lot in common," he smiled. He had a nice smile. His whole face lit up. I studied him. I looked at his body language. "C'mon, I'm harmless," he said as he shrugged his shoulders. He *was* cute. Rick had really light brown hair and green eyes. He was tan and muscular.

I imagined him carrying me out of a burning building. I imagined other things too. It's still hard not to picture every guy *naked*. I know, I know – shame on me. There he was, standing only a couple inches taller than me, with a cocky grin on his face. I always liked guys that were a little cocky.

I unlocked my Corvette and sat down, then unlocked the passenger side. "Get in," I told him. Then we drove down to the beach.

We went to Maurice's. He was my father's best friend. We were seated in my usual booth, which is in the back of the restaurant so no one bothers me. When we were done with the menus, I looked at him and he was smiling at me.

"What?" I asked.

"I can't believe you're not married, especially since you're burning with passion and everything." He took a sip of his tea.

"You know too much," I said.

"Well, you're not shy about expressing yourself, are you?"

"It's not like I was planning on dating anyone from the group. I thought it was like a support group," I said, innocently.

"What, for horny Christians? I think that group meets down the hall," he said, laughing.

I laughed too.

"The good news is, I think I understand how we can cause other people to sin," I said.

"Oh, trust me; you know how to cause other people to sin."

"Did you watch *Tom & Jerry* when you were a kid?" I asked him.

"What? Are you kidding me? That was my favorite cartoon." Rick said.

"Do you remember when Tom or Jerry would have little angels and devils on their shoulders?" I asked.

"Yeah, I remember."

"That's how I feel," I said. "I mean, I've been who I am all my life and now I have to be a totally different person."

"I thought everything would be easier, but it's not!"

"I can't believe how honest I'm being with you."

"I'm glad you feel comfortable enough to talk to me."

"I shouldn't. I don't even know your last name."

"It's Sullivan. What's yours?"

"Pagano."

"Italian, huh?"

"Yeah, my dad's side. My mom was Irish."

"Irish/Italian – that's quite a mix. So, I'm betting you know how to cook?"

"Yes. I'm a really good cook," I said.

"I love Italian food. You want kids? Because I'm ready to marry you right now," he said.

"Can't have 'em, actually," I said apprehensively.

"But do you like kids?" he inquired. He didn't seem to care that I couldn't have kids.

"Um," I looked around, deciding how I would answer him.

"Because I have two."

"Oh. That's nice."

"Did I just go down a couple of notches?" He looked a little anxious.

"No. I think kids are great."

"Really? You're not convincing me."

"Sure. I would make an awesome wicked step-mother." He threw back his head and laughed. "Truth is," I continued, "I grew up in a very small town and we didn't have relatives in the state, so I was never really around kids."

He pulled a picture out of his wallet and gave it to me.

"This is McKenna and Pete."

"Oh, they're so cute. How old are they?"

"She's eight and he's six."

The waitress came over with a refill of tea, and I thanked her. I asked Rick if the kids liked living in Florida and he explained they were still in Connecticut with his ex. He told me his dad lived down here and has a bad heart. Rick was an only child, so he had to move down to take care of his dad. He said he wished he made more money so he could get his father better healthcare.

Rick didn't really like Florida and said he'd rather still live in Connecticut, but his father loved it and didn't want to leave. He said he felt bad for saying it but he didn't think his dad would live that long and he just wanted to make his dad happy.

"It must be hard for you to be away from your kids."

"Hell yeah. I hate it. And I work such a complicated schedule being a fireman; I'm on for twenty-four hours and then off for forty-eight."

"So, you're not even working the same days every week?"

"No. It makes it impossible to get a second job, too."

"Wow, that makes it hard to take care of your dad. Or have a relationship – I would imagine."

"Yeah, it's complicated." We both fell silent. It was comfortable though, not like with some people where you're nervous because you can't think of what to say next. "So, Megan, what's your story?"

I didn't think I was ready to, but I unloaded my whole sad story. I left out the part about being wealthy. I told him about the diner and he said he'd check it out sometime. We got very personal with each other. I asked him what happened with him and his ex.

"Our problem was she didn't like to be alone. That's not good when you're a fireman and you can't be home every night." I just nodded. "I should've known right from the beginning, it wasn't going to work."

"Sorry, that sucks."

"Yeah, I thought it was weird, our neighbor kept fixing all the stuff that was wrong in our house. I didn't know he was fixing it up so he could move in!"

I told him we tend to miss a lot of warning signs when we love someone. Rick said they had been together since they were fifteen years old. I can't imagine being with anyone so long! We left the restaurant and walked on the beach. We walked for miles. He had a very self-deprecating sense of humor, which I loved. We talked for hours.

He took my hand and I noticed how rough it was. I hadn't held a blue-collar hand in a long time. There was something very comforting about him. I didn't know why, but I felt safe with him. He walked me back to my car and asked, "May I kiss you?"

"Do you think I want to kiss you?"

Rick gave me a lopsided grin. "You'd be crazy not to want to kiss me."

I laughed. "Well, I don't want you to think I'm crazy." And, he kissed me. He was a good kisser. This guy was definitely going to be good to kill some time with.

"I still have to drop you off at church," I said.

"I know, but I wanted to kiss you here. I didn't want to make out with you in the church parking lot," he said. We laughed together. I had little butterflies in my stomach.

"Can you imagine Andy walking out and seeing us kissing in my car?" I asked.

"He'd probably have a heart attack."

"At least you know CPR!" I said. We got in the car and drove back to the church parking lot. It was so late I was glad his car didn't get towed! We made plans to go to a movie the next day. I programmed his number into my cell phone and he kissed me one more time.

Then we said goodnight and he got into his car and drove away. It had been a long time since I dated a guy who drove a Honda! It would be good to get back to a simple life with a normal guy.

Maybe because he was like the guys I used to know in Massachusetts. He was honest and real. And the best part was – he had no idea I was rich. He just liked me, for me. That hadn't happened in a very long time.

We spent every day he had off, together. I appreciated the fact he didn't take life too seriously. He was exactly what I needed. It was going so well after a month, he wanted me to come down to the fire station and meet everyone. I told him I would bring them all lunch.

I decided to take my Ford F-150. I still hadn't had 'the talk' with him about my money. I made it a point to meet him wherever we went, or he would come to the diner. He had no idea I lived in a mansion. When I got out of the vehicle, they all came out to greet me. Rick kissed me. I noticed some of the guys looked at me strangely and talked amongst themselves as they walked towards us.

His captain, Tom, came up to me and extended his hand. "Nice to meet you, Megan."

"Hi," I said as I shook his hand.

Rick was clueless, poor guy. It was clear all these guys knew who I was. One of the firemen, John Evans, came over quickly and started aggressively shaking my hand.

"Hi, you're even prettier in person," he said, gushing.

"Thanks," I said reluctantly, looking at Rick.

Rick was taken aback by this. "John, what do you mean *in person*?"

"She's in all those articles in the newspaper. You didn't tell us you were dating Megan *Pagano*. Ka-ching!" he said, like he was motioning a slot machine.

"Am I missing something?" Rick asked me.

"Yeah, like the fact you're dating 'The Lottery Heiress!'" John said.

The other firemen started staring at me like I was a wax figure that was amazingly life-like. I just gave them an insincere smile. They encircled me like I was a freak show.

"Can I speak with you?" Rick asked me. "Why don't you guys get the food?" he hollered to his co-workers, "We'll be right back." He gently pushed me into an office. The guys weren't shy about going into my truck and grabbing the food I had brought.

"So, you're 'The Lottery Heiress?'"

"I am."

"Is there anything you want to say to defend yourself? Obviously, you didn't trust me enough to tell me who you were."

I looked at him. Boy, he really looked mad. I've never been good at getting out of trouble, so I just told him the truth with a smile. "I love you!" I said, as I kissed him. He kissed me back.

"You love me, huh?"

"I do," I said sincerely as I looked deeply into his eyes.

He looked at me seriously. "Then, why have you let *me* pay for everything?" He asked with a smile.

We got engaged six months after we started dating, but he didn't want any part of the money. Oh, he didn't mind when I paid for dinner occasionally. And he liked driving all my cars – except the Corvette. I didn't let anyone drive it.

I finally persuaded Rick to let me hire someone to take care of his dad, but I spent time with Jack myself, too, and we became good friends. I checked on him at least every other day. He told me I was the daughter he always wanted. He had great stories, too.

He fought in Vietnam and worked at the Pentagon. He was rich with history and he also had a great sense of humor – I could see where Rick's came from. But he was so lonely. Rick's mom had died from a rare form of cancer and Jack never remarried. She had been gone about ten years when I met Rick.

I was getting ready for a weekend with Rick. We were going to spend the weekend in Naples. We had made plans to stay at The Ritz-Carlton and check out locations for our wedding reception. We had been looking forward to this trip for weeks. Rick's schedule was more screwed up than ever because of budget cut-backs, and he would not let me help him out financially. So he had to switch his hours around to get the time off. Finally, he had it all arranged and I was excited to have these four days together.

But Rick called while I was at his dad's house. He told me he was taking his friend's shift. He asked if I was mad, which I was, but I knew he wanted to work. I never met anyone like him.

He didn't want me to support him, and all I wanted to do was make him quit so we could travel, or get a house in Connecticut so he could see his kids. Whatever he wanted – I just didn't want him doing such a dangerous job for such low pay. I told him I understood, but I was not happy about it.

Before we hung up, I told Rick how much I loved him.

I turned to Jack and asked him, "I don't suppose you'd like to go Naples with me?"

He grinned at me. "I'd go to the moon and back with you." I laughed and hugged him. Yes, really, I hugged him. He was an awesome guy.

We were watching *Wheel of Fortune*, yelling letters at the television, when my phone rang. I saw Rick's picture and said "Hi, sweetheart."

"Megan, it's Tom."

"Oh, hi Tom. I thought it was Rick."

"Are you at Jack's?"

"What? Yeah. I'm here."

"Come to the door."

Almost before I was on my feet, the knock came.

I opened the door. A few of the other guys, including John, stood there with Tom. I knew something was wrong. They were covered in ashes and sweat, and they still had their gear on.

"Megan, you need to have a seat."

"I don't want to." Maybe there would be no bad news if I stood up.

"What's going on?" Jack asked as he wheeled himself over in his wheelchair. Tom looked like he was about cry. The other guys turned their faces away from me.

"There was a call tonight. It was a bad one. I called everyone out of the building, but Rick didn't make it out. I'm so sorry."

Jack screamed. I've never seen a grown man cry like that. I didn't even move. I didn't cry. I didn't even hear what they were saying to me. I just kept looking at Jack. I walked out of the house. John followed me.

He tried to comfort me. I kept saying the word 'no.' John tried to hug me, but I pushed him away and I yelled, "Get away from me."

All I could think was maybe God wants me to be alone. Maybe he's punishing me. But I was good this time. I didn't even have sex with Rick. We were actually waiting until we got married. What did I do to bring this curse on myself?

Knowing Jack would need me more now than ever, I went back into the house. Jack grabbed me so hard by my arms, he almost pulled me down. He was sobbing so hysterically that I couldn't deal with it by myself. I asked Tom if he could stay for a little while, and he did. But it was terrible. I had to be the strong one, and I felt so weak.

Another funeral – that's what kept going through my mind, *another* funeral. And I really loved this man. He loved me for who I was. I would never find that again. That kind of love comes along only once in a lifetime.

The funeral came and went. Through it all, I was numb. You never get used to mourning and loss. You shouldn't have to.

I asked Jack to move into my house. I didn't think either of us should be alone. I was worried about who would take care of him without Rick. He said yes.

One night, not long after he moved in, he called me to his room. "Megan, would you mind going to the convenience store and buying me some lottery tickets?"

"Are you kidding me, Jack?"

"Wouldn't it be great if I could just live off lottery winnings?" he asked.

"Um – you do."

"No, I mean, wouldn't that be neat?" he asked.

"Yes. It would also be like, statistically impossible," I said.

He waved the money at me. "Please, just grab me five quick-picks, okay?" he asked. I stared at him for a minute, thinking about what it would look like if anyone saw me buying them. But it was such a small way to make him happy. I grabbed the money and told him I would be right back.

I got in my R8 – first mistake. I didn't wear a hoodie or a wig – second mistake. And I chatted with the clerk long enough to have someone recognize me and take a picture of me with their smart phone and send it to Joseph Carr. That was the third and worst mistake of all.

The next day, instead of waking up to winning lottery numbers for Jack, I woke up to this headline: "Lottery Heiress Spending Inheritance on Lottery Tickets!" The subtitle read, "When will enough be enough?" Jack saw me reading the article in the kitchen and he felt so bad.

"I am so sorry, Megan," he said.

"It's not your fault, Jack. I should've sent someone else. I should know better by now."

He only lasted nine months after Rick died. But I think he enjoyed the last part of his life. At my house, he had every luxury he could ever want. And he agreed to go to church with me. That was something he would never do with Rick. He made a lot of friends. He was like fresh meat for the older ladies at church. They loved him!

It was a shame he died so soon. We had become so close. It was nice having a dad around again. Now I had to get used to being alone – again. To make matters worse, James informed me he was moving to Hawaii to be the bodyguard for some television star. I knew better than to ask what else could go wrong.

For the next two years, I faithfully went to church every Wednesday night and Sunday. I even joined the choir. I read my Bible every day and learned about self-control and restraint, two things I was never good at. I threw myself into every activity I could to distract myself from the pain I had suffered over the years – even the pain I brought upon myself with my lifestyle.

I learned what it means to be a Christian, and even how to deal with the hypocrites in the church. Unfortunately, there were a lot of them. You know the type of people, they seem 'perfect' on the outside and they are judgmental of everyone else. Me, I've got nothing to hide. I let everyone know I'm screwed up and I still struggle not to do the things I've done all of my life.

Not all the people in the church are happy with me. It is daily battle for me to be a better person. I wrestle with almost every decision I make. Recently, this young woman in the church got pregnant – out of wedlock. What a scandal! Even worse, I suggested to the women in the women's Bible study that we should throw her a baby shower and some of them responded by saying, "But – she's not even married!"

I stood right there in front of them and said, "Didn't Jesus say something about people without sin being the first to cast stones? I guess that's you guys, huh? I thought we were supposed to show the world Christ's love. If we can't even show it to someone in the church, what good are we to the rest of the world?" And I walked away.

That didn't go over very well with a few of the church

ladies. But most of them agreed we should do something. I called The Ritz-Carlton in Naples and threw a huge baby shower for her. Both she and her mother were very grateful. And of course, those nasty ladies came too, the ones who didn't want to do anything for this poor girl.

I'd assumed everyone in the church was loving and their goal was to be more like Christ. I was wrong. That's probably why so many people don't want to have anything to do with church nowadays. I wonder what the world would look like if the church just loved people. I wonder what our own country would look like if the church was doing what it was commanded to do.

I never was concerned with the way people felt about me. Like I said earlier, people either love me or hate me, there is no in between. But given the way my life changed with the money and the church, I decided I would find something nice to say about everyone I met. That would be my way of reaching out to people who didn't like me.

And I try not to say anything bad about anyone – you know, like moms used to say, "If you don't have anything nice to say, don't say anything at all." I am convinced if people still used this rule today, no one would say very much. Finally, I resolved not to retaliate when people said cruel things about me. I was determined to find something positive in everyone – not an easy task.

I continued my self-improvement by becoming a black belt in karate. I pulled out my old guitar, which hadn't been touched in 15 years, and started playing again. I joined a country club and took golf and tennis lessons. I took some classes at the local college. I had to fill my mind.

I didn't date much after Rick. If I did, I made sure the men were not attractive. I had made a covenant with God. Now I had to live by the Bible, which means no getting drunk, no cussing, no sex, etc. Since those were three of my favorite things, they were the hardest for me to abandon. I reminded myself constantly that God had a plan for my life. And I replaced my old, fun habits with a new one – over-eating.

I packed on 30 pounds within a year! But cheesecake and potato chips and ice cream made me happy, though the feeling was short-lived. As soon as I stepped on the scale or walked into my closet filled with designer clothes I couldn't wear anymore, I regretted my gluttonous lifestyle. I'll never forget the article Joseph Carr wrote about my weight gain, "The Lottery Hogess." I loathe that guy.

I woke up one day and knew immediately something was wrong. Really wrong! I couldn't feel my fingers or toes. I was peeing every 20 minutes. I felt nauseous. I was thirsty and no matter how much water I drank, I couldn't get enough.

It felt like I was drinking all day and night – but I wasn't. I'd noticed over the last couple of weeks my memory was slipping. I dreaded going to the doctor, but something was wrong with me. Would I be next?

I got to the doctor's office. I was listening to my iPod and reading a magazine to appear normal, but I was freaking out. The nurse came and brought me back to the examining room. She asked me a lot of questions and then the doctor came in. I have known him for years.

"Hi Megan." He shook my hand. "What is going on with you today?" I told him all of my symptoms. "Well, I think we'll get a urinalysis and take some blood. No fever or vomiting, right?"

"No. I feel great, other than all those symptoms." He chuckled. I did not.

I peed in a cup and put it in the little cabinet. Why would anyone want to work in healthcare? I am grateful people do, though.

After about five minutes, the doctor came back. "You have ketones in your urine."

"What does that mean?"

"I think we need to have you go downstairs to the lab and we will check your sugar and insulin levels. You probably have diabetes."

"I can't have diabetes – *I'm pretty.*"

He laughed. "Yeah, unfortunately, that's not the way it works."

"What does this mean?" I asked.

"Your organs are turning on you. I'm sure we caught it early enough. You just need to lose thirty pounds and you need to exercise. Have you ever thought about working out with a personal trainer?" I just gaped at him. "You also need to follow a strict diet. Of course, no processed sugars and limit your carbs."

Limit my carbs? I *am* part Italian. No spaghetti with garlic bread? No cannoli? No fettuccini Alfredo? No New York style cheesecake? What a sad, sad day. Oh, what about pizza? I can't live without pizza. That's just barbaric. *That's un-American!*

I have diabetes. How is this possible? I grabbed the papers he gave me and started walking out. "Have a nice day." I grumbled.

I gave them some blood and went home. When they called the next day, you guessed it, they confirmed what they thought. I thought I had to be huge to get this disease. I knew people twice, three times my size who don't have it. My mom had diabetes too and was never bigger than me. I guess I just thought I was invincible.

I finally decided to trade in another bad habit for a good one. I really didn't have much choice. I had a gym in my house and I never even used it. So, I hired a personal trainer and I decided I was never going to be fat again. To my surprise, sugar was a lot like men.

Once I cut them both out of my diet, I didn't really notice. But if I was around either one of them, there was a potential for danger. I realized I had to take care of myself because no one else would.

I was really depressed because I hit that age. You guessed it, thirty. There is such a stigma attached to that number when you're unmarried. Everyone says it's when your body starts changing. The way I looked at things changed, too.

For example, when I was in my twenties, I got really offended when people would say I had a boob job. I have always been small and had big boobs; I can't help the way I was made. Now that I was in my thirties, when people say I got a boob job I know the girls have held up pretty well – no pun intended – and I am not offended anymore. Now, I'm flattered. How sad.

I was supposed to be married by now. I'd been so close, twice, and had lost them both through no fault of mine. It seemed so unfair and I didn't understand it at all. I reminded myself it was God's will and if He wanted me to wait for the right one, then that's what I wanted to do. But, honestly, sometimes I didn't mean it sincerely.

Sometimes I felt sure Rick *was* the right one and something had gone wrong with God's plan. I wondered if I would ever be with anyone again.

It's been two years since Rick and I were engaged and I became a Christian. That's right, two-and-a-half years since I've been with a man – you know what I mean. Did I mention it's been a long two-and-a-half years? Now it's two weeks before my birthday.

The town is buzzing about a movie being filmed on Fort Myers Beach, right down the road from my house and diner. Yeah, it will bring money into the town, but they are getting permits to block streets and otherwise annoy the people that live and have to work here. And here's the bonus, it's starring Mark Taylor. Yay. My buddy. I hope I don't run into the man again. Oh well. Life goes on. There was a definite need for some excitement in this town.

It was the beginning of July. I drove my Corvette to the driving range at my country club and parked way out in the middle of nowhere so no one would mess with my car. After putting my make-up on in the parking lot, I walked into the club thinking it would be like any other day. I waved to the golf pro, Ted, whom I have taken many lessons from. The range was almost about to close, but he always lets me come late so people don't bother me.

I was just minding my own business, whacking my bucket of balls, when I felt someone staring at me. I looked up and noticed it was none other than Mark Taylor. He was working with Ted on his swing. Mark grinned at me and waved. He leaned on his club for a dramatic pause. I just raised my eyebrows and gave him a look that said, 'I'm not interested,' and looked away.

I kept feeling him look at me. Ugh. When I was down to my last ball, I put it down on the green and lined my driver up with a little wiggle. Just then, Mark Taylor walked by me wildly swinging his golf club like an idiot, striking me on my head, knocking me out. When I woke up several minutes later, my face felt funny. Apparently, my face broke the fall.

Luckily, there were plenty of doctors working on their golf swings. I woke up to find one taking my vital signs. Ted was kneeling over me too, asking if I was all right.

"What happened?" I asked them.

"Mark Taylor accidentally hit you and knocked you out," the doctor said.

Once you've had one head trauma, you become a hypochondriac with any injury to the head after that. But the doctor said I was going to be fine.

"Do you want me to drive you home?" Ted asked.

"Yeah, okay. I have a headache. I'll have a car service drive you back here," I said.

Ted took the keys and helped me into the passenger side of my car. I moved the rear view mirror to look at the damage.

"Oh my gosh, look at my face," I said, touching the swelling around my right eye and temple.

Ted started up the car. "Don't worry. The doc said if you keep that ice pack on your face you should look normal in a few days."

"Mark Taylor is such a jerk," I said.

"He looked like he felt bad," Ted said, defending Mr. Taylor.

"He took off awful fast for someone who felt bad," I snipped.

"Well, there was a crowd forming."

"Yeah, I guess people wanted to see if I was okay?" That made me feel better.

"No, people heard Mark Taylor was leaving and everyone was trying to get his autograph."

I *really* dislike Mark Taylor.

CHAPTER 5

Two weeks later, it was my birthday. I sprang out of bed and decided to eat a huge breakfast at the diner. I hopped in the shower and went to my closet. I decided to wear something really cute, and do my hair and make-up nicer than normal.

I might be a year older, but there was no need to feel any worse than I already did. I walked down to the garage and tried to decide which car I would drive. I pointed at all of the keys hanging up and decided on driving the Corvette.

I parked my Corvette right in front of the diner and went inside. Everyone yelled, "Happy birthday, Megan."

"Thank you," I said. Amy came over and I had to fend her off. "I don't need a birthday hug, Amy. But thank you." Everyone laughed.

The patrons in the diner were talking about the movie production and how it was messing up traffic. All the blocked lanes and detours sure had slowed me down this morning. Amy swore she saw Mark Taylor jogging in front of the diner earlier that morning.

He was fresh off a hit movie where he played a Marine

in combat, *Mortar Man*. Everyone got excited because they might get a glimpse of a movie star. I, obviously, did not share their enthusiasm.

Mary and Carol handed me their gifts and asked me to open them. Amy came running over with another package. "Happy birthday!" Amy said to open hers first. It was chocolate tea.

"Wow. Two of my favorite things together. Brilliant. Thanks, Amy. That's why you're my favorite employee."

"Really?" she asked.

"No, but it was a good gift." Mary asked that I open hers next. I ripped off the paper. It was a huge bottle of hand sanitizer. "Thank you, Mary!" I said, sincerely.

"You're welcome, Megan. I went to BJ's Wholesale Club so I could get the big one. We all know how much you love washing your hands. You probably should've been a surgeon." She rolled her eyes.

Okay, so I have a little Obsessive Compulsive Disorder. Do you know how dirty people are? Gross. I seriously don't like getting slimy or hot or dirty. Every time I shake someone's hand, I run to the bathroom and wash my hands. I don't think it's weird.

I don't know where their hands have been. My O.C.D. got worse after I started watching *Dr. Oz*. But I didn't watch him for long – I kept getting the symptoms of whatever he was discussing. I was driving everyone at the diner crazy, so they asked me not to watch him anymore!

Carol rubbed her hands together. "Go ahead, open mine."

"What is it?" I opened the box. It was a cameo that had been in her family for generations. "Oh, Carol, I can't take this."

"Please, Megan. My sons don't care about it. And you're more like a daughter to me than their wives are."

"Are you sure?"

"I am absolutely sure, Megan. I know you will appreciate it and those girls sell everything I give them on eBay."

"Thank you all so much. I will treasure this, Carol."

"I know, honey," she said.

Mary said, "I didn't know what to get. What do you give a pretty, rich girl? A handsome, rich guy?" We all laughed.

Bud handed me an envelope. "This is from me, Megan." It was a gift certificate to a day spa. "And, they have one of those organic lunches included, you know, so you don't have to add any more empty carbs to that big butt of yours," he said with a laugh.

"Thanks, Bud. But it's rude to point out other people's flaws, you short, bald, fat man," I replied. It's good to laugh on your birthday.

Mary handed me an invoice. "I know it's your birthday, darlin', but Juan sent over the invoice and it's screwed up again." Juan was a salesman for the food supplier we used and he screwed up our invoices on almost a weekly basis. I didn't think it was an accident. I think he was trying to get me to overpay on purpose because he knew I had the money. I threatened him last week and told him not to screw up the invoice again.

"Is he trying to lose us as a customer?" I asked, aggravated. "Well, I will deal with this on Monday. I want a relaxing day with no worries. Put on some Jimmy Buffet," I said to Amy.

She turned on the jukebox and I went in the back office to put the invoice on the top of my inbox. I sat down, looked around to make sure the coast was clear. I opened my desk drawer, and pulled out the engagement ring Rick gave me and tried it on. Carol came to the door and caught me with the ring.

"How are you doing?" she said.

"I'm fine. Another year older, but I'm okay. I felt good this morning. I woke up and thought 'I don't look bad for my age,' considering I'm in my 30s, still unmarried, with no prospects. I put on these jeans and thought I looked great until I turned around and saw huge panty lines."

"So?" Carol said.

"So – I'm not *wearing* any. Maria went back to Colombia for two weeks to visit her family. I'm running out of laundry."

"Megan, I have a radical idea."

"Go shopping?"

"No. Do your own laundry."

"That's just crazy talk. And I don't want to go shopping for underwear. I think my body is changing. I remember when I used to have a butt that wouldn't quit." I said.

"I had one of those, too. It was forced into early retirement." We both laughed. Then her face got real sober. She pointed to the ring. "Seriously, how are you doing with that?"

"I'm okay. It's been two years. I was just thinking, two years ago, I was sure I'd be married by now. Every time I get close to someone, something happens."

"I'm sure Rick wouldn't want you to feel bad on your birthday, Megan."

"I know. I had a dream about him last night. Things just don't work out the way you think they will, you know?"

"Do you think I wanted to spend my golden years as a waitress, widowed two times, with arthritis, scraping by on social security and a *pathetic* salary?"

"Hey!" I snapped.

She laughed. "No offense. Just trying to get your goat."

"I just thought my life would be more exciting. And it *is* my birthday. I was hoping something interesting might happen."

"You never know what's in store for you. Your life could change in a moment." She gave me a sympathetic smile. I nodded.

"I'm sorry I have to go to my sister's tonight. Otherwise we could do something fun," Carol said.

"It's all right. I know Dave isn't doing well. I just can't believe I have to be alone on my birthday. It sucks."

Dave was Carol's brother-in-law. He was in renal failure and we all knew it wouldn't end well. I wondered if it was easier to lose someone the way I did, suddenly, without warning, or knowing it was going to happen. Either way, it's the worst thing to happen to a family. I prayed for a miracle, but it would never come for him. I wondered why some people get healed and others die.

"C'mon, Megan. Stop feeling sorry for yourself because you don't have a date on your birthday. Poor little pretty rich girl." She chuckled. "It's kind of hard to feel sorry for you from where I am standing."

"Oh well. I guess I'll just grab some sushi and watch a movie." I watched Carol pace back and forth across the room.

She told me something that surprised me. She said Phillip came by. It had been a long time since I'd seen him. I assumed Melinda was with him since they wound up getting married. Carol told me they got divorced. I said I was sorry to hear that, for the kids' sake.

He actually asked her if I was dating anyone. What a laugh – like I'd even consider being with him again. I did ask how he was aging though and Carol said he looked good. Phillip told Carol he had something he wanted to give me. I wondered if it was the money he borrowed all those years ago.

Amy ran into the office all excited. "Megan, your favorite actor is here – eating in the diner! And he's asking for you."

"If Cary Grant's out there, that will scare the crap out of me." Carol and I laughed.

"No, your favorite *living* actor," Amy huffed.

"Liam Neeson is eating my eggs!" I exclaimed. "Ugh, that sounds gross."

"Yeah, it does," Carol said. Carol and I started walking down the hall.

"No, it's not Liam Neeson, it's *Mark Taylor*," Amy squealed with delight.

"Ugh. What does he want? Is he finally going to apologize for knocking me out at the driving range?"

"I don't know, but he's asking for Big Mama."

Carol and I exchanged a glance and said at the same time, "He wants the Corvette." My dad had a personalized plate on the car that said, 'Big Ma' and I had kept it all these years. I told Carol I didn't want to talk to him, but she made me do it anyway.

He was better looking than I remembered. But then, this was the first time I'd seen him up close when he was conscious. Then he knocked *me* out and *I* was unconscious. So, this was really the first time I saw him up close with both of us being conscious. But however handsome he might be, I still wasn't interested.

"Can I help you?" I asked. I hardly recognized him in his hat, sunglasses and goatee. I still hate facial hair. It wasn't even groomed. It looked as though a baby ferret was sitting over his mouth with its little tail curled up. Gross!

"You can't be Big Mama," he said as he took off his sunglasses.

"That's just the name of the diner, *obviously*."

"Oh." Then he smiled. "That's your Corvette?"

"You mean the one that's not for sale? Yes."

"You may not know this, but I'm an avid car collector and if there's one car I need, it's the *1963 Z06*." He smiled again, arrogant, like I was supposed to swoon into his arms.

"If I were to sell my car, which – spoiler alert – *isn't* going to happen...I wouldn't sell it to the guy who knocked me out at the driving range!" His eyes widened.

"Hey, that was an accident," he added defensively. He made eye contact with Eddy and stared at him for a couple of seconds.

"Nice. Now, if you'll excuse me, I have important things to do." I walked into my office and shut the door with a snap. Then he opened my office door to find me playing Scrabble on the computer.

"Don't you knock?" I said angrily. "You can't just barge into someone's office."

"Look, I didn't know that was you at the driving range."

"You could've asked who I was and apologized. I've been going there for years."

"There's no excuse for that except I've been working since I got here. So, I'm sorry." He looked sincere, but he's an actor, so it was hard to tell. He plunked his butt down on the corner of my desk. "Do you forgive me?"

I looked him up and down. "I guess so."

"Good. Now, what's it gonna take to get me in this car today?" he said with a sly smile.

I looked at him in disbelief and sighed.

The smile disappeared from his face. "Can I ask you a serious question?" I raised one eyebrow. "Why is there a retard in your restaurant?"

I sat back and crossed my arms. "Good question. Why are *you* in my restaurant?"

"Not *me*." He pointed back toward the dining room. "That guy out there, clearing tables."

"Eddy has Down syndrome. What's your excuse?"

Mr. Taylor frowned at me. "Hey, I think we got off on the wrong foot here."

"What's your problem? You can't take no for an answer?" I added. I turned back to the computer.

"Women don't usually say no to me." He was actually surprised he didn't get his way.

I laughed. "*I* am saying no to you, ferret face."

"Why would you call me 'ferret face'?" he asked looking bewildered.

"Because facial hair is disgusting. Especially the dead animal *you're* wearing." He touched his face. "Look, Mr. Taylor, no one around here is impressed by you. People here aren't shallow and caught up in celebrities."

I walked out of my office and into the dining room. He followed me.

"Can I buy you dinner?"

"You don't get it, do you? Just go away."

"You're cute when you're angry. C'mon, any woman in town would have dinner with me."

A female patron yelled, "I'll have dinner with you, Mark." He nodded and waved at her.

"See? Stop playing hard to get." Bet he thought he was winning me over.

"Okay, if you stop playing hard to want! My dad left me that car when he *died*."

"Come on!"

"Just go away!" I snipped.

I thought he was looking at my boobs, but I guess it was my shirt. 'Tuesday is Soylent Green Day,' it read.

"Great t-shirt," he said. Did that line work with other women? How pathetic. "Soylent Green is one of the greatest classic movies of all time!" Like I didn't know. "There's no one like Charlton Heston."

I nodded. "All the great ones are *dead*."

And he agreed. "He was King."

Huh. He knew I was trying to slam him, yet he agreed. Brilliant. Well-played.

I lectured him, going on and on about how Fort Myers Beach was a family town and had old-fashioned values and we didn't care about Hollywood or celebrities. Unfortunately, one of the patrons had already posted all over social media that Mark Taylor was in my diner. By the time I pushed Mark to the door, a crowd had collected on the sidewalk. He went out and signed a bunch of autographs, then used my car – *my* car – as a backdrop for the photos all those fans wanted. What a jerk!

I set off the car alarm with my remote. He looked in the window and saw me holding the remote. What was wrong with this town? Why did they care about Mark Taylor? I hadn't even seen one of his movies – well I saw one, but it was a cartoon. I don't think that counts. What a bunch of hoopla over nothing. And what an ego! How dare he think he could come in and charm his way into getting my car.

Once the alarm sounded the crowd dispersed pretty quickly. Then, I had to contend with customers and employees scolding me for my treatment of a 'celebrity.'

Heaven help me, he came back into the diner. I was standing at the serving counter looking through my mail. I didn't even bother looking up.

"Sorry, sir, the restrooms are for patrons only."

"I came back to give you one more chance to make your dreams come true."

"Nightmares," I said, quietly.

Carol couldn't keep quiet any longer. "Just go, Megan. It is your birthday, and it's not like you have any plans." I shot her a nasty look.

"Is this true?" he asked. "You don't have plans? You would rather be alone on your birthday than go out with me?" He put on a big act, all sad and rejected.

"Awww," everyone said.

You could see the confusion in his eyes. Apparently he didn't know how to deal with rejection. Was there ever a woman who didn't fall all over him? Everyone in the diner was telling me to go out with him – right in front of him.

I could've killed them for that! I tried to explain to Mark Taylor several times we didn't have anything in common, but he couldn't get it through his thick, wavy hair. It looked really soft. He was actually pretty cute and I *was* having fun messing with him.

"I am not leaving until you agree to have dinner with me."

"Let's walk outside, Mr. Taylor. Excuse us, everyone."

"Nice to meet you all," he called out as he followed me through the door.

"Why are you pushing so hard?" I asked.

"What's the worst thing that could happen?"

"I could actually *like* you."

"Look, I don't know anyone here, I hate eating dinner alone and it *is* your birthday."

"So I'm doing you a favor now?"

"I'll be back at five."

"Perfect, I close at two."

"Wait a minute, then you won't be here at five!"

"Wow, you're sharp."

"Fine, then I'll wait in your car until you leave and then I'm buying you dinner."

"Good grief, I'll meet you back here at five. But *now* I have to have lobster."

Mark shook his finger at me. "I knew I'd get you to say yes."

"Trust me, Mark, I will say no to you. And I'm a black belt in Karate. No means no."

"Apparently not when dinner's involved," he said with a chuckle. I just shook my head. I was sick of arguing.

"I'll see you later," he said. As I watched him walk away, I thought, if I could just give him a lobotomy he'd be perfect. The outside was nice to look at. He had one of those smiles – you know, the kind that spelled trouble. It was clear why he was voted 'The Sexiest Man Alive.' In any case, he is a total jerk. How can anyone call Eddy a retard when he is so sweet?

Everyone wanted to know what we talked about outside. They were curious how I got him to leave. I just told them I'd asked him to come back another time. That wasn't a *lie*, but I definitely omitted some of the details.

No one needed to know he was coming back to pick me up. Nothing was going to come out of dinner anyway.

I told Carol I was going to the spa after work. She raised an eyebrow at me. After the spa, I went home and put on a black t-shirt and jeans, and black high-heeled sandals. I wasn't going to get dressed up for this guy when I knew it wasn't going anywhere. I slipped my license into my back pocket so I wouldn't have to carry my purse. I got back to the diner just before he did.

When he came back at five he had on dark jeans and a tight black t-shirt with expensive Italian shoes. We looked like twins. He had shaved his goatee; he had to get rid of it anyway for the movie. It was a *huge* improvement, but I pretended I hadn't noticed.

"You look nice," he said.

"Thanks," I said. He lifted his eyebrows, expectant, like he was waiting for a compliment. He even pointed to himself. I gave in. "And you could look worse."

He laughed. "Wow, that was painful, wasn't it?" I giggled.

"Can I drive?" he asked hopefully. I could not believe his audacity. I never let *anyone* drive this car, not even my fiancée. Well, I did let Ted drive it, but that was when Mark knocked me out. It certainly doesn't count.

He held his hand out for the keys and smiled mischievously. "I shaved for you." He grabbed my hand and brought it to his face rubbing it across his chin. "See?" I reluctantly placed the keys in his hand.

"Got you to say yes again," he crowed as he got into the driver's seat. He put the keys in the ignition and revved the motor.

"Do you want to kiss me yet?" he asked.

I looked him up and down. "Definitely not!"

He threw the car in gear and hit the gas. He sped past the entrance to the Matanzas Pass Bridge that exits the island. He was driving way too fast for the main beach road.

"Can you please slow down? I don't want you to kill a pedestrian with my car."

"I can't help it, this car is fast!"

"And, how far are you going?"

"How far are you going to let me go?" He slapped my thigh and then left his hand there.

"Not far, Mr. Taylor." I picked up his hand and dropped it back in his lap. He laughed.

"Where shall I take you for dinner?" he asked.

"Do you like seafood?"

"I love it."

"I know where to go, just follow this road for about a mile. It'll be on the left."

The more I examined him, the better looking he got. His dark hair was a little longer than it should be. He had perfect bone structure and intense eyes. And perfect teeth. I am all about the smile. What would it be like to kiss him? He was probably a terrible kisser. I'd gone out with perfect looking men before, and they always seemed to disappoint. Not much danger of that with this one since my expectations were so low.

But he had cute little earlobes. I could just imagine nibbling on them – like thousands of other women, no doubt. He must work out a lot 'cause it definitely showed. I guess he would have to. I liked the way he dressed, too. I had to keep reminding myself this was the guy who threw up on me, and then knocked me out at the driving range. And now he's the guy who wants my car.

Not to mention he kisses people for a living. Ugh. That

is so repulsive to me. I don't even like sharing TIC TAC mints out of the container. How could anyone get involved with someone who kisses other people and does love scenes for a living? No thank you. Relationships are already hard enough. You hear about actors falling in love on the set all the time, even when they're married. Why couldn't he just be an accountant?

Plus, he's a drinker, which is dangerous for me to be around. Not to mention sexy, which is *really* dangerous. Why was I over-analyzing everything? I told him where the restaurant driveway was. He pulled in, parked, and then came over quickly and opened my door for me. We started walking across the gravel driveway to an inconspicuous entrance used only by employees. The building was gray and looked like an oversized beach cottage. It was right on the ocean and the fresh catch was always literally just caught.

Mark looked around. "This doesn't look like the entrance."

"It's not, but I always go in this way. I know the owner."

We arrived in the upstairs dining room and Maurice saw us. He motioned us to my regular booth and came over with our menus. "Happy Birthday, Megan." He kissed my cheek.

"Thank you," I said. Mark stood up to shake his hand.

"Maurice, this is…"

"Please, I recognize the star of *Don O'Malley*. Nice to meet you, Mark."

"Hi Maurice."

"Megan, I didn't know you were dating Mark Taylor."

"Well, it comes as a shock to *both* of us," I said. Mark scowled at me.

"Can I get you something from the bar, Mark?" Maurice said.

"Oh, I don't drink," Mark said. "Can I just have a sweet tea?"

"Make mine un-sweet please, Maurice."

"Sure, I am going to leave you lovebirds alone. I'll send your waiter back with the drinks."

"You stopped drinking?" What a surprise that was!

He pointed and scolded me, "You don't know me. You think you know me because you read in a tabloid magazine I was in rehab a few times?"

I touched his hand. "I'm the one from Mason & Mason who found you."

He sat back, a look of dismay on his face. "Oh my God. No wonder you didn't want to go out with me."

"It's not just that. I don't date celebrities."

"I'm not who I used to be."

"Neither am I," I said as I smiled at him.

The waiter came over to take our order and left quickly. "What do you think the odds are you would be the same person in Miami, at the driving range and with the Corvette?"

"I don't even know. Sounds like the worst luck ever!"

He took a sip of iced tea. "So, did you grow up in Florida?"

"Massachusetts."

Then he did what everyone always does when they find out I'm from Massachusetts, they say "Park the car" in a horrible Boston accent. Again, in a horrible accent, he said "That's a wicked good candy bar!"

"Are you done? Have you noticed I don't speak like that? Most people from Massachusetts speak without an accent. That's really a coastal accent you're mocking."

He paused and examined me. "You're really pretty."

"Well, I wasn't always this pretty."

"I didn't think so. What did you have done? Your nose? Your lips?" He looked at my chest. "Your…"

"Don't even say it!" I snapped.

"Seriously – have you had any work done?" he asked.

"Yes, I had my kitchen renovated," I said, sarcastically.

He laughed. "I meant, you know, cosmetically," he said.

"I had braces – that's it. I am 100% natural, unlike the people you know."

"You're a lot more sarcastic than the women I usually date."

"Please don't compare me to the Barbie Dolls you date."

"That's not fair to compare the women I date to Barbie Dolls."

"I'm sorry, you're right, Barbies don't have enough plastic."

Mark laughed and then acted offended. "I'm sure I'm not like the typical guys you date, either."

"No, I prefer Italian men."

He asked sincerely, "You think they're better lovers?"

"*No!* They always know where to get good pizza."

He laughed. "So, what are you looking for in a man?"

"He has to have a good sense of humor, and be kind, and work boots wouldn't hurt."

"Work boots? Really?"

"Oh yeah, when I see a guy in work boots, I know everything's going to be all right."

He said straight-faced, "You know, you kind of remind me of my high school girlfriend."

"Oh, she didn't like you either, huh?" I laughed.

"No, she also had dark hair and green eyes."

"Was she Italian?"

He smiled. "You're Italian?" he asked.

"Only half," I added.

"Which half?" he asked.

"The bottom," I said. He spit out his drink in laughter.

I really caught him off guard. He lifted up his napkin.

"Oh, I've got tea coming out of my nose," he said, dabbing his nose with his napkin.

I laughed. "Sorry," I said – even though I wasn't. It was really disgusting, but funny. "My dad's parents were from Italy," I added.

"I love Italy. In fact, I'm going there in a couple of months to shoot a commercial for Ferrari – which is so weird, I swore I'd never do a commercial, but I had this dream and I knew I was supposed to go."

"What – you had a dream about the commercial?"

"No, I had a dream, I was walking with this beautiful woman and I just kept hearing the name 'Pagano.'" I looked at him in disbelief.

"What?" he asked. So, I pulled my license out of my back pocket and showed him. "Look," I said.

"Wow!" he said. I thought he was remarking about my last name. "Is that your real age?" he asked.

"Look at my last *name*," I said.

"Yeah, that's weird." He said as he handed my license back to me.

The waiter came with our food and I prayed before I took a bite.

He smiled. "Huh, I haven't seen anyone do that in a long time."

"Let's just assume I'm *a lot* more old-fashioned than

the women you – we'll call it 'date.'" I made quotation marks in the air.

"Good. Maybe that's what I need."

"I doubt I'm what you need, Mr. Taylor."

"I can't believe you're not married."

"I was engaged to Phillip Mason."

"Really? He's too old for you. You need someone like me, young and full of stamina!"

"Wow, is it getting hot in here?" I asked hoping I wouldn't need a cigarette before the end of dinner.

"So, what happened with you and Phillip?"

"We found out I couldn't have kids right before the wedding."

"That's harsh."

"It gets worse; he dumps me literally minutes before I find out about my parents' accident. Then, I met a great guy named Rick."

"What happened there?"

"He was a firefighter. He didn't make it out one night."

"I'm so sorry."

He tried to change the subject. "So, are you an only child?"

"I wasn't. My older brother enlisted after 9/11. He died fighting in Iraq."

"I don't know what to say right now." He smiled sympathetically and leaned in to me. "Am I going to die before dessert?"

"I hope not, I didn't bring my wallet," I said. Mark laughed.

We chatted through dessert and coffee. Mark placed a small velvet box in front of me.

"What's this?"

"It's your birthday present."

"Oh, you didn't have to do that."

I opened the box. They were large diamond and sapphire earrings set in platinum. They were something I would've picked out. They were beautiful. He asked me to put them on. I told him I had a gold allergy and he said he knew because he had called Carol after I agreed to go out with him to ask what he should get me.

She is such a stinker! She didn't say a word, but it explains why she was smiling so mischievously at me when she left work. When I put them on, I asked him how they looked and he said, "Good." Then, he reached out to touch my left ear and smiled at me.

Mark went to the restroom, and I looked at my watch. I guess I hadn't been paying attention, because we had been there for three hours! When he came back to the table, a man and woman followed him.

"Hey, man. I don't mean to interrupt your dinner with your girlfriend but can you just say the line from *Don O'Malley*, please?" Neither of us corrected the guy about the girlfriend comment.

Mark smiled. "Sure." He exhaled and stretched his arms out in front of him and got an intense look on his face. "I've always wanted to be a one-woman kind of guy, but then again, I was never any good at math."

The guy laughed and asked Mark to sign a napkin, which he did. The woman he was with was just standing there giggling and finally mustered up the courage to tell him he was even better looking in person. I realized I was starting to like Mark when I just wanted this woman to leave so I could talk to Mark some more.

I asked Mark if it was hard to have a relationship in his business. He said it was, because he never knows if someone wants him because of his personality or just because he's rich and famous. I guess we weren't so different after all. I was so tired of men wanting me for my money. I couldn't believe I was actually enjoying dinner with Mark Taylor. I wondered what else I'd enjoy with him!

Mark told me he had changed a lot since reaching his thirties. He said when he was younger, he'd just pick up any woman he wanted, but now he was ready for more. I told him I used to enjoy picking up men, but I kept getting hernias. I expected a laugh there, but nothing! Tough booth!

Maurice came back and said he picked up the tab. We thanked Maurice. Mark left a huge tip for the waiter and we left. We decided to take a walk on the beach towards the pier.

"So, do women think you're like the characters you play?"

"Yeah. A lot of women don't care about getting to know the real me. Sometimes, they're actresses who just want to use me to help their career or girls who just want to get into the best night clubs."

"You're not really like Don O'Malley, are you?"

"No! That guy was a jerk. I'm nothing like him."

"I heard it was a good movie, though."

He stopped in his tracks. "Wait a minute, are you telling me you didn't even see it?"

"Nope."

He was in shock. "It made $400 million worldwide. It's a modern day classic."

"I don't watch R-rated movies."

"Why?"

"I have enough R-rated thoughts in my mind. I don't

need someone else's."

That intrigued him and he wanted me to expound upon my R-rated thoughts. He told me he took some psychology classes in college and offered to help me work them out, or *act* them out. I laughed and declined his 'help.'

Mark put his hands on my waist and asked me if I wanted to lie down and look at the stars. I told him we could as long as he promised not to get fresh. I hate lying in the sand, but I was having a good time so I ignored the sand getting in my clothes. "Isn't that sky amazing?" I asked. There were more stars than I ever remembered seeing before.

"Yeah, it's perfect." He was looking at me, not the stars, so I knew I was in trouble.

"Look, Mark. I'm gonna be real honest with you. I know you don't know me, but I just tell it like it is, okay?"

"Okay." He backed off.

"Much to my surprise, I actually liked being with you tonight. But I'm in my thirties and I need to get married."

"Are you being deported?"

"No." I let out a laugh. "Look, I've read about you and I won't waste my time with a Hollywood playboy who just wants to screw around. I'm looking for more than that. So, I wish you good luck with your movie and your life but I'm not gonna have a meaningless relationship with some hot famous guy just to be tossed aside when something better comes along."

He sat up and grabbed my hand. "I don't expect you to understand this because you're not a celebrity, but people write things about me that aren't true. I'm actually a pretty decent guy. You only know the Mark Taylor the media tells you about. You should take a chance and get to know the real me. Did it ever occur to you maybe I'd like to get married too?"

"No, it did not."

"Do I think I'll find the love of my life in Fort Myers? Probably not. But I'm open to it. I will settle down when I meet the right person," he said.

Something was stirring inside of me and I knew it was dangerous. I hoped it was just food poisoning and not the fact I was making grand plans in my head with this guy I hardly knew. We made plans to see each other the next night. He said he would take things slow just to prove he was a nice guy. I told him he was going to *eat* those words. We walked back to the car and got in. He tried to kiss me but I put my hand on his chest and sighed.

"I don't kiss on the first date," I said.

"Okay."

"It's been a long time since anyone has kissed me."

"Why?"

"I don't kiss just anybody."

"Lucky for both of us, I'm not just *anybody*."

I went to work the next day with a smile on my face. That made everyone suspicious.

"Good morning, everyone."

"Wow," Carol said with a smirk. "You're very chipper for someone who spent their birthday alone."

"Well, I think you know I *wasn't* alone last night," I said.

Carol played dumb. "Oh? Who were you with?"

I just squinted at her, shook my head and waved my

index finger as if to say 'no.'

"Did you see the article Joseph Carr wrote about you today?" Carol asked.

"Now what?" I asked.

Carol read the headline, "Lottery Heiress Goes Ballistic on 'Mortar Man' Star." Then she threw the paper down on the counter.

I picked it up, "Hey, that headline's actually funny." I read the article out loud. It said I verbally assaulted Mark at the diner, in front of a large group of his fans. Then it went on to say the movie he was in was expected to pump hundreds of thousands of dollars into our economy and because I was worth hundreds of millions I didn't care about the little people in the community who would benefit from the production. "Absolute trash!" I said as I threw the paper down on the counter.

Carol gave me a sympathetic smile and told me not to let it bother me. I just didn't get it – why was Joseph Carr still writing stupid crap about me? I was relatively boring now compared to how I used to be. I worried Mark would see the paper and know how much I'm worth. Before I could finish the thought, a flower delivery guy came in the door.

"Is there a Megan here?" he asked.

"I'm Megan," I said. Bud tipped the guy, while I signed his log and grabbed the card. I laughed when I read it. The card read, "Roses are red, violets are blue, I'm a nice guy and I'll prove it to you! – Mark."

Everyone asked who they were from. I wouldn't tell, but I read his poem.

Carol laughed. "Wow. You got a real Walt Whitman on your hands there, Megan." She grabbed the card out of my hand.

"Carol, if you read that card out loud, they'll have to notify your next of kin," I threatened.

Bud said, "That's pretty dramatic, Megan."

"No, this is dramatic." I shook the card. "You will have to pry this card from my cold, dead hand." I saw the smug smile Carol had on her face and I turned toward the door. There was Mark, coming up the steps to the diner.

The first words he said were, "Good, the flowers came." Everyone looked at me with their eyes wide open and their mouths agape.

Mark came up to me and put his arms on my waist. "What time can you get out of here?" I could feel myself blushing as everyone stared at us.

"Come here." I grabbed his hand and walked him outside. "I kind of didn't tell anyone about us." I said.

"Oh, sorry. Are you embarrassed?" he asked.

"Embarrassed? Please. Look at you. No, I'm not embarrassed. It's just…" I added quietly, "I don't have the best luck with the people I date, so I try and keep it on the down low."

"Too late for that. What time can I see you?"

"Do you want to meet me here at 2:00? I promised Carol I'd close for her today."

"Sure. I'll be here."

I hugged him and when I pressed up against him, I smelled him. I thought I did it discreetly, but apparently not. I couldn't identify the smell but it certainly was *manly*.

"Did you just sniff me?" he asked with a surprised smile.

I tried to be cool about it. "Yeah, I just wondered what cologne that was."

"You like it? It has pheromones in it. It's supposed to

make me irresistible."

I took another whiff, shut my eyes and exhaled. "I hope you can get your money back," I said as I tried not to lick his face.

He kissed me on my cheek and we said our goodbyes.

He drove away and I walked back inside. Everyone scattered away from the window.

Bud leaned close to me and said, "Watch yourself with this one."

"Is he a good kisser?" Carol asked. Amy and Mary leaned in to listen.

"I didn't kiss him yet," I said.

"But you wanted to?" Amy asked excitedly, as she put on her lipstick and put it into her apron.

"Are you blind?" Mary snapped. "There's enough heat between them to melt your hooker-red lipstick."

"Oh, it's not hooker-red, Amy." I said.

"Then you don't deny it? You want him?" Mary beamed. "I knew it."

"I smell love in the air!" Amy said excitedly.

I sniffed. "I think that's bleach."

I left the diner and went shopping. I bought a nice new outfit and prayed for strength. I wanted to hold that first kiss off as long as possible, determined not to do what my flesh wanted. How should I work 'the talk' into the conversation? When and how do I tell this guy I won't have sex until I'm married?

We were talking about an international sex symbol here. He could walk into any place in the world and go home with someone. What could I offer this guy that would keep him interested? I may as well tell him tonight so I can just pick up and move on...again.

I went back to the diner and ate the daily special, which was 'The Lord is my Shepherd Pie.' Carol asked me if I had heard about some new church motorcycle gang. I had not. I laughed at the idea of it. "They should call themselves 'Heck's Angels,'" I snickered. "They could have t-shirts that say 'Born to be Mild.'"

"You never know, maybe I'll meet my next husband through it," she said.

"Maybe," I said.

Bud chirped up. "Carol, I could always take you out if you want some company." Carol and I looked at each other. That was the nicest thing I had ever heard Bud say. He added, "I'm just saying..."

Carol grabbed her purse. "All right, Bud, I may take you up on that sometime," she said. "See you later, Megan."

"Bye, Carol," I said as I leered at Bud. "You are quite the ladies' man, Bud."

"Oh, put a sock in it, Megan," he said.

I tried to call Cindy but she didn't pick up her phone. She was going to freak out when I told her about Mark. I was wiping down the tables and counters when Cindy called me back. She was a psychologist in private practice, but she also worked part time at a hospital in Miami. And at night, she was trying to make a name for herself as a comedian. Her husband was not happy about it.

I answered the phone. "Hey, lady."

"Hi, did you have a nice birthday?" she asked.

"I did. Are you working on a Saturday?" I asked.

"Yes, and I hate my job so much. All my patients do is

cry and tell me all their problems."

"They didn't warn you when you were getting your degree in *counseling*?"

"What a nightmare. Everyone in my office is looking to change careers. I hope this comedy thing works out. So what are you doing tonight, Megan?"

"I'm going out with Mark Taylor," I said casually.

"Hold the phone, are you kidding me?"

"No. He came into the diner yesterday and we totally hit it off."

"Yummy! Did you kiss him?"

"You know I don't usually kiss on the first date."

"That's not a rule you keep for *Mark Taylor*. That's a rule for the ugly dorks you usually date."

"Nice, Cindy. You know, some of those dorks are nice people."

"They have to be because they are so *ugly*; they have nothing else going for them."

"You know, not everyone can marry a rich executive."

"Well, he's married to his job now, I hardly even see him," she said.

I knew she was excited and wanted to talk, but I had to get ready. "I really hate to say this, but I have to go. Mark is coming in a couple of minutes to pick me up."

Cindy warned me not to screw things up with Mark. She wanted it to work out so she could meet him. She was a huge fan and had seen all of his movies. She wanted to know if he looked as good in person as he did on screen. I told her he looked better than when I'd seen him on television.

She thought I was crazy for not kissing him and made me promise to call her as soon as I did. Then, she asked me to text a picture of him without his shirt on. I asked her why his shirt would be off. She couldn't think of a good reason, but she thought of several *bad* ones. She was always my worst influence, but no one else makes me laugh harder than she does.

I looked at the clock, counted the deposit and put it in the safe. It was 2:00. I changed my clothes, re-applied my make-up and did my hair. I looked out the window, grabbed my purse and locked the door.

CHAPTER 6

Mark got out of his car and gave me a smile I knew was going to be the end of me. He walked up to me and announced, "It's our second date." I opened my mouth to say something, but he grabbed me and kissed me. I mean one of *those* kisses.

Like old Hollywood movies, where you knew the characters were in love before they did. It was an amazing, amazing kiss, the kind people write about in romance novels. No one had wasted that kind of passion on me in a long, long time.

He looked at me and touched one of my ears. "You're still wearing the earrings." He held me at arms' length and said, "What do you want to do?"

I couldn't shake off that kiss. I felt blurry and warm and I couldn't comprehend what he just asked me. I felt as though I had been drugged. Everything moved in slow motion.

"I'm driving, right?" I gave him my keys. As soon as he turned away, I took a couple of steps back and slapped my right cheek really hard. We got into my Corvette. I'm sure I had a handprint still on my face.

"No one has ever kissed me like that before."

He grinned and winked at me. "I know. I was saving that one for *you*." He said as he patted my thigh.

"Let's just start driving and I'll tell you where to go," I said. Boy, was I in trouble.

I asked him about the movie he was shooting. He said it was about the Buckingham Air Field, which was used to train gunners in World War II. Like I didn't know! "Have you seen the airfield yet?" I asked.

"No. They're going to use sound stages to shoot those scenes. The weather is too unpredictable down here. Why, do you know where it is?" he asked.

"Yes. We're going to go for a little ride." I said. "My great uncle on my dad's side trained as a gunner at Buckingham Air Field."

"Really?" he asked, interested.

"Yup, but he died in the war. He was shot down over England."

"Wow. That's too bad," he said.

While we drove, he told me the film was a love story about a lieutenant and a civilian set in the '40s with the war story in the background.

"I bet you have some cool costumes," I said. "I think it would have been so neat to live back then."

"I don't know. They used to have air raid drills and make kids get under their desks. I don't think it was any better than it is now."

"Well, maybe just the romance of the decade. The music, the clothes, the expectations. It was just a slower pace." I pointed down a little road. "Take a right here."

Mark asked why I had a house so far away from the diner.

"I don't. I have a house at the beach, but I'm not sure

I'm ready to let you see it yet."

"Megan, I don't care if you have less money than me."

"Huh. I feel the *same* way," I laughed a little, nervously.

We pulled into a modern subdivision with beautiful homes and perfect manicured lawns. The only thing that made this subdivision different from others was the oversized garages.

"What is this?" he asked, looking around at the large homes with huge garages.

"Just pull in to that driveway," I said. We got out of the car and knocked on the door. Marilyn Walters answered the door.

I made the introductions. Marilyn and her husband were a sweet couple I knew from church. "Hi Megan," she said. Then she looked at Mark and clapped her hands over her mouth. "Oh my goodness, you *are* the 'Sexiest Man Alive'!" she said with a giggle.

We went into the house. She shouted for her husband, George.

He came over and saw me, "Hi Megan."

"Hi, Mr. Walters, I brought my friend over to meet you," I said.

"Hi, I'm Mark Taylor," he put his hand out.

"Well, I'll be; you're famous! I'm George Walters."

"Yes, sir. Nice to meet you," Mark said as they shook hands.

"Mark's making a movie about the Buckingham Air Field. It's a love story set during the Second World War," I said.

"I was stationed here then," George said.

"I was hoping you could take him around and show him where everything was," I said.

"Oh, I'd love to. C'mon, let's take my golf cart," he said.

He gave his wife a kiss and he told her he'd be back later. Mark gave me a kiss. When they walked out the door, she looked at me and asked me to explain why Mark Taylor was just in her living room!

She made us some tea and I told her the whole story – going all the way back to Miami. When they came back, Mark was pumped up about the stories George had told him. He felt they would give him more depth for his character.

George had shown him where the hospital was and the old mess hall and sleeping quarters. Mark told them it was a pleasure to meet both of them and he shook their hands.

He thanked George for taking the time to show him around and telling him about his time being stationed there.

I hugged them both and told them I would see them at church. We walked out to the car. I took the keys from Mark's hand and started driving to the river house, where I kept my seaplane.

"Thank you, Megan."

"You're welcome. And listen, I have a plan for dinner. Trust me, it'll be something different."

We arrived at the river house and pulled the car into the garage. We walked right to the back dock. The dock shook while we were walking on it. The plane started to rock back and forth in the water. This did not help convince Mark that it was safe.

"Ta dah!" I said as I showed him the plane.

"Oh *no*, I'm not getting in *that* thing!" he said as he pointed to the plane.

"C'mon, it'll be fun. I'll take you to Captiva Island. I know a great restaurant there. You'll love it!"

"How long have you had a pilot's license?"

I looked at him seriously. "License? They don't really enforce that, do they?"

"Not funny, Megan," he said, backing up. I grabbed his arm and walked him to the plane.

I opened the door to the plane and crawled in. "Get in!" I yelled. I started the engine and put my headset on, then patted the seat beside me.

I convinced him. He got in the plane and sat down but he wasn't happy about it.

"Trust me," I said. "Buckle up and put your headset on."

"I'm a celebrity, don't crash."

"Hey. If we crash, you'll be immortalized forever."

"Too bad I'll be dead and miss it."

He buckled up and put his headset on. Mark looked at me like he wanted to change his mind, so I started moving the plane before he could.

We taxied down the river and lifted off. I banked the plane and smiled. I was having fun making him nervous. He wasn't cocky now!

"Oh, God," he said.

I tried to sound wise, "Many a man has found religion on plane."

"I just want to find a barf bag," he said, looking queasy.

I laughed. "I've logged over 3000 hours. I've been flying for years. You don't need to worry. I wouldn't let anything happen to you."

We flew to Captiva Island. It was only about twenty minutes away. I landed the plane in a little inlet behind a secluded restaurant where only millionaires and celebrities go. We coasted to the restaurant's huge dock. A porter from the restaurant came and opened the plane door for us. He tied the plane down for us and we tipped him.

"Have a pleasant evening, folks."

We went up to the hostess and she seated us in a booth in the back corner. We saw other famous people there with their families and the people who were not famous didn't bother the celebrities. Mark loved it. After dinner, we took a walk on the beach. There were a lot of regular people there.

"Why aren't people asking me for my autograph?"

"It's no big deal. We see a lot of celebrities down here. I mean, we have the Red Sox down here for Spring Training, and countless celebrities buy homes on Sanibel Island and in Naples."

"Is that how you met Mike Sanders?"

I stopped walking and looked at him. Mike Sanders was a pitcher for the Red Sox that I had a brief fling with.

"Ted told me."

"Remind me to smack him," I said as we continued down the beach.

"What happened with you two?"

"Um, he didn't recycle." I wasn't about to tell him it was because I wouldn't have sex with him.

He started questioning me about my relationship with Phillip. He said he didn't understand what I saw in him. I told him it was security and because he was older, he made me feel safe.

I also told Mark that I liked the places Phillip took me, like The Breakers in Palm Beach, the parties in South Beach and the vacations in the Bahamas. It occurred to me then that maybe I never liked Phillip very much at all.

"You know, every guy I've ever been with has wanted to change me?"

"And every woman has tried to change me. But, I am who I am."

"I guess we'll know we're with the right person when they *don't* try to change us."

Mark asked me, "Now, if you *had* to change one thing about yourself, what would it be?"

"That's easy, my breasts."

His eyes widened and he looked at my bosom. "You'd make them *bigger*?"

"No, but why am I not surprised that you went there? I would make them prettier. They're ugly."

"Ugly?"

"Yeah. I mean, I went to bed one night in fifth grade flat as a board and woke up with a 'C' cup."

"You must've been pretty popular."

"Not 'til high school. But they are just ugly. I mean, at least they look good with clothes on."

He nodded in agreement. "They certainly do." I smacked his arm and he laughed. Then he said seriously, "I'm going to do something for you."

"What?" I asked, knowing he was up to no good.

"I think it's important you get an objective opinion about them. You should show them to me. I'll be honest with you."

"You know what? That's *never* going to happen! What about you, Mr. Perfect? What would you change about yourself?"

He stopped walking for a moment.

"I have a bump in the middle of my nose. It looks huge from certain angles. You can't really see it until you look at my side profile. See?" He looks at me dead on and then shows his profile from the side.

"Whoa. Careful with that thing. You're gonna hurt someone." We started walking again.

"Oh, come on."

"Honestly, Mark, you're still perfect!"

"Perfect, huh?"

"I mean – you're still a lot less ugly than most people."

"Uh huh!" He turned to me and took my hands. The water lapped over our feet.

"I'm having a really good time with you, Megan."

"Me too."

Mark leaned in to kiss me and a pack of young male yuppies passed by. Their apparent leader yelled, "Yeah, get some, Mortar Man. Woo!" The rest of them laughed and whooped.

He waved at them and kissed me.

We held hands as we walked back to the plane. We took off for the beach house, talking about the history of Fort Myers as we flew. I was nervous about him seeing my house. I didn't know how he was going to react. I assumed he would be relieved that I didn't care about his money.

"Are you ready to see my house?"

"Sure."

"Don't be weird about it, okay?"

"I promise. I won't."

After about ten minutes, we landed to the east of my beach house, on the canal. He looked at the house with confusion. We coasted in and I parked the plane at the dock and opened the plane. We hopped out. I tied the plane down and started walking towards the house.

"Wow. That looks like a really nice guest house. How'd you manage that?" Mark asked.

I laughed, "I don't live in the guest house."

"Are you house-sitting?"

"Nope." I walked a step ahead of him.

He looked up and saw the security guards on the roof. He grabbed my arm and pulled me to the ground behind my thatch tiki hut in the garden. "Who are those people on the roof?" Mark asked nervously.

"That's my security team but don't worry; they won't shoot you unless I tell them to," I said as I got up. He got up too.

"Oh my God, you're a mafia princess! Your parents' accident was really a mob hit! That's why everyone around you dies!" he said.

I laughed. "No! But that's way more interesting! Don't worry about them." I said, pointing at the men on the roof. They waved at us. We went into the house.

He looked around the house with amazement. He wandered here and there, picking up my stuff and inspecting the artwork on my walls. He handled everything very carefully.

"So, you don't need to work?"

"Not anymore. My parents had money."

"I thought you were poor. I thought you were embarrassed about where you lived."

"I *am* embarrassed. I mean, my parents were blue-collar people most of their lives. I'm still not used to this." I gestured around at all the stuff.

"Neither of my places are this big," he said as he looked at many framed letters and pictures on my wall from politicians and famous people.

He was surprised how many people I knew. I told him I do a lot of charity work and it kind of goes with the territory. He went from picture to picture like he was in an art gallery.

He stopped at a bunch of photos of a woman on a car – a woman he clearly didn't recognize. He was amused. I touched one of the pictures. "Oh, Boo." I closed my eyes.

He looked at me and raised an eyebrow. He really wanted to know why I had pictures of a woman straddling a Bugatti.

I slapped his arm. "That's me, and I'm not *straddling* it!" I sighed. "Man, I loved that car. And people hated me for it."

"Why is that?"

"Uh, it was just a car," I said casually, trying to act like it was no big deal. "I know, it's stupid, they're just machines. But when I drove that car, it was as if we became one," I said.

He just smiled. He saw my mom's baby grand in the main living area. He sat down on the bench and asked if I played, but I never learned how.

He asked if I minded if he played. I told him to please go ahead and play something. He started playing "You're the One." That was the title track from a love story he starred in.

"Do you know this song?"

"Yeah, it's from *You're the One*. I never saw that."

"That's not surprising – it *was* rated R. Did you know I wrote this song?"

"No, I didn't know that."

"It was number one for seven weeks."

He started singing. It was a duet.

"I would tell you to chirp in, but I'm sure you don't sing."

I smiled and he continued with the song. When it was over, we just sat at the piano.

He kissed me and said he wasn't surprised I knew that song because I seemed like the 'easy listening' type. I laughed and immediately grabbed his hand and led him to the music room in my house. It was soundproofed like a real session room and filled with guitars, amps and drums.

To say he was shocked would have been an understatement. I told him I had to run and cut my nails real quick. I hadn't played guitar in a few weeks. I went to the bathroom and clipped my nails down. When I came back, he was sitting in one of the chairs in the studio, just waiting for me to amuse him.

I picked up a guitar and lifted the strap over my head. I took the pick out of the strings and turned the amp up. I started playing "Ain't Talkin' About Love" by Van Halen.

That was the first song I ever learned how to play, and I told him so. I played about half of the song and he came over and stopped me.

"I think I love you," he said as he planted a very passionate kiss on me.

He grabbed a guitar. "May I?"

"Absolutely," I said, trying to shake off the distracting kiss.

We jammed for a little while. We both took turns playing songs we knew. We sat down on the amps. Mark was impressed. We were both sweating a little bit. I opened a fridge in the room and threw him a bottle of water.

He asked if I ever thought about playing in a band. I told him I was in an all-girl band in college but I had a problem at the radio station I was working at and I decided not to pursue music, or radio for that matter.

He inquired further and I pulled my shirt down off my shoulder and up my side to show him the scars from where a stalker had stabbed me.

"Oh my God."

"Yeah. I decided I didn't want a life in the public eye. I made a deliberate choice not to pursue fame and fortune. I value my privacy and safety."

"And now you're dating me?"

"If I didn't like you, you wouldn't be here. And the money's just made me more paranoid. Honestly, sometimes I go for days without leaving the house."

I pulled my favorite guitar off the wall.

"What are you doing?"

"Singing a song to you," I said. I lifted the strap over my head and sat on my amp.

He didn't think I was serious. "You told me you can't sing."

"Actually, *you* said I couldn't sing!"

I started playing the guitar. I sang a song to him that I wrote and he laughed.

He sat there just smiling at me. Then he came over and kissed me and I got nervous.

"Want to shoot some pool?" I asked.

"Sure."

We walked down the hall to the game room. He laughed at my huge velvet painting of dogs shooting pool, hanging next to the pool table.

"Nice painting," he said sarcastically.

I pretended to be offended. "I commissioned a very

famous painter to do that."

He looked at me in awe. He couldn't believe it.

"I'm just messing with you. I bought it at the flea market for fifty bucks!"

He smiled. "Right, because the original is in the Guggenheim." I smacked his arm and laughed.

We played some pool. He kissed me, long and hard. I didn't think about how long it had been since I ate something. I felt like I was going to pass out.

I told him I was tingling and I felt weak. He said he was too, referring to our kiss. I giggled and asked if he was diabetic too.

He grew concerned and I asked him to take me to the kitchen. We took the elevator up to the kitchen. I ate some food while he just stared at me. I was kind of embarrassed.

"I'm quite a catch, huh - endometriosis *and* diabetes."

"I still think you're a catch, even with all your diseases," he said sincerely.

"Wow, you know what a girl wants to hear," I said, thinking he didn't realize how that sounded.

"That kind of freaked me out. I mean, what if you were driving or flying and that happened?"

"I usually wear a watch that beeps every couple of hours to avoid doing…that."

"Why didn't you wear it today?"

I showed him my wrist. "Rolex. Curse you, vanity!" I shook my fist.

He was worried I had to take insulin or medication. But I reassured him I can control it by diet and exercise. I tried to convince him I just lost track of time and I never get that bad.

"I mean – it's fine. Like, I don't pass out or anything."

"I was worried about you."

"I'm embarrassed to tell you this, but normally, I'm here or at the diner. I don't really do anything. I lead a very boring life." I looked at Mark. "Well, it *was* boring; I can't say it's been boring for the last couple of days!"

I went to use the restroom, and I returned to find Mark reading the newspaper at the kitchen counter. He looked at me while putting one hand on his side and tapped his hand on the counter.

"Oh crap," I said, knowing how rich people *despise* lottery winners.

"You're this person?" He asked as he pointed to the article. "You're 'The Lottery Heiress?'"

I sighed and looked him straight in the eye. "Yup, I didn't want to tell you because people get weird when they find out."

"Megan, I don't care. I liked you when I thought you were just a slacker with a diner. I like you even more now."

"Well, that's the problem, Mark. Everyone likes me more after they find out I can buy my own country."

He slammed the paper down and jabbed his finger at the article. "See this? I don't care." He flung it aside. "I wanted you before I knew this. Frankly, I'm relieved you don't care about money."

He took both my hands and looked into my eyes. "You could give it all away and we live on my money alone, and I wouldn't care."

"But you're only worth about $17 million. We couldn't even buy Rhode Island with that!"

He laughed and kissed me.

"How do you know that?"

"*Please!* I always investigate people who want to get close to me."

"Well, I don't think you're different from anyone else."

"Really? How much money did you make last year? I mean – I already know, but I'm asking you for dramatic effect."

"About seven million."

"Wow. That's more money that most people make in their *whole* lives, and you made it in one year."

"Yup," he said proudly.

"That *is* impressive. But I made $16.9 million dollars last year – *in interest.*"

"I'm not just saying this, but I swear you just got prettier!"

I told him I'd trade it all in a heartbeat to find someone who would love me for me, and not my money.

"Megan, I don't give a damn about your money."

I smiled, but I felt like crying. "Tell me you're not too good to be true."

"I'm not if you're not." He touched my face with his right hand and kissed me very tenderly. Then he caught sight of the clock on the wall. "Hey, it's 3:00 in the morning! I'm supposed to be on the set in an hour!"

"You're going to be exhausted."

"I wish I had my car here. I don't want you driving this late."

"You ride motorcycles?"

"Yeah."

"I have a Ducati in the garage."

"You have a Ducati? I'm *serious* – I think I love you.

Do you mind?"

"Not at all."

We went out to the garage. I switched the light on and the first thing he saw was the Audi I got carjacked in on a turn table. "You've got to be kidding me," he laughed.

Then he saw my small car collection, including some exotic cars but also my pick-up truck, and my Ducati. He raised his eyebrows. I shrugged my shoulders. "You're a piece of work, Megan." I handed him a helmet.

He grabbed the helmet and then he kissed me. It was quite a kiss. He sat down, put the helmet on and put the face shield up. Man, he looked good on my bike. "I'd like to come over tomorrow when we wrap up," he said.

"You better! And, drive carefully."

"I will."

He lowered the shield again and I opened the garage door. He drove off. I walked to the end of the driveway to watch him. I heard him accelerating. He was going fast. It scared me. Not the rate of speed, because Lord knows I like to drive fast.

No, the fact I'd met a male version of me, which scared me. He couldn't be this good. This couldn't be as good as it seemed. There had to be *something* wrong with him.

I looked up to the sky and clasped my hands in prayer. "Oh Lord. Please don't let him die on my Ducati. Please, Lord. It's okay if it doesn't work out. But please don't take him, too."

I woke up about 9:00 the next morning, showered, and made some breakfast and coffee. Then I decided to go to the diner. When I got there, Bud was telling Carol about a motorcycle accident that happened around 4:00 down the road. A car hit a motorcycle and both the drivers were killed. I went wild.

"Who was it? I have to know, Bud. Tell me what you know, now!"

"The names haven't been released," Bud said.

"What's the matter, Megan?" asked Carol.

"Mark took my bike around 3:00 this morning. He had to be on the set at 4:00."

They all looked concerned when they saw how hysterical I was getting.

I put my hand on Bud's shoulder. "Bud, please call one of your friends. I have to know."

Bud excused himself and went outside. I could see him moving his arms. It seemed like he was out there for a very long time. He came back in.

"It was a 16-year-old on a joy ride. He stole the bike."

"Oh, thank God," I said, as I sat down and put my head in my hands. When I looked up, I realized someone was still dead. I didn't mean to be so insensitive.

Everyone looked at me.

"I'm sorry. I'll pray for his family."

"Megan, can I see you in your office?" Carol asked. We walked into my office.

"What is going on with you? You seem very tightly wrapped for just a couple of dates."

"I know."

"What is this guy doing to you?"

"I don't know."

"You need to slow down, Megan."

"I know. I know. You think I like feeling this way? I'm totally out of control. I can't stop thinking about him.

This was not in the plan. A celebrity? What am I doing? When he touches me, I feel like I'm going to spontaneously combust. That doesn't really happen, does it? I hope it's just an urban legend. Because I swear, it's gonna happen." I put my hands on my head. Carol laughed.

"Wow. You're totally in love with this guy. You've only been on two dates with him!"

"I know. It's crazy. It's crazy." I exhaled. "Carol, this can't be happening, I can't be falling for him this fast. I mean, I can't be in love with someone this fast. Does real love happen this fast?"

"Oh honey, it did with both my husbands." Carol had had her bad luck with love too. Her husbands died from heart problems. Carol must be some kind of *wild woman*!

I reminded Carol about my coma and Jesus saying he was going to send someone I was not expecting. I asked her if she thought it could it be Mark.

She told me I was a 'goner,' and I'd better hope this guy was everything I was building him up to be or I was in for the disappointment of a lifetime.

I knew she was right, so I decided the right thing to do was pray on it. She rested her hand on my shoulder and closed her eyes. I asked God to reveal the truth to me. I asked him to show me who I was supposed to be with.

A second later, someone came rapping on the door.

"It's Mark."

I looked at Carol. "That's good enough for me!" I said as I opened the door.

I went up to him, and kissed him long and hard while Carol snuck out of the office.

"Wow. That was quite a greeting," he said with a huge smile. He was still holding me.

"There was a motorcycle accident this morning. I thought it was you!"

"No. I'm fine." He said as he touched my hair with his right hand.

"What are you doing here?"

"My co-star's drunk again. She's totally incoherent. The director's not too happy. She keeps delaying production."

"What's her problem?"

"It's not all her fault. She *was* a Disney child star."

"Oh!" I said sympathetically. "Do you want me to drive you home?"

"No, I'll be all right. It's just down the road."

"Okay, but be careful."

He kissed me. He started walking out of the diner. He said goodbye to my co-workers and I walked him to the bike. He put the helmet on.

He lifted the visor and said, "I can't stop thinking about you, Megan." He sat on the bike, turned the engine on and drove off.

Mark called about 3:00 and asked me to go over to the beach house where he was staying at 4:00. He said he wanted to cook me dinner.

He left the door unlocked and couldn't hear me knocking because the music was so loud. I startled him when I just walked in. He saw me and yelled, "Jesus Christ!"

I pointed behind me and shouted back, "Is he behind me again?"

"What? No!" he said, confused. He went over to the

stereo and turned it down.

"Then, let's try and not break any more commandments tonight, okay?" I said.

"I can't promise that," he said. Unfortunately, *neither* could I.

I went over and kissed him. "Something smells great." I asked if I could help. He said no, but it looked like he was preparing a pretty complicated meal.

He'd crushed some pistachios and was flattening chicken breasts. I smiled while I watched him. I couldn't remember the last time a man cooked me a meal.

He coated the chicken in the pistachios and threw them in the oven. He set the timer, then washed his hands and started chopping up salad greens.

"Where did you learn to cook?" I asked.

"My roommate in L.A. was a chef. He taught me how to cook because I was too broke to ever go out," he said, smiling. "Starving actor, right?"

"Not anymore! Did you keep in touch?" I asked.

"No, I wonder whatever happened to him." He threw the greens in some bowls and started cutting up more vegetables.

We talked until everything was ready. He said that it had been a really long time since he had made dinner for anyone.

He told me that he's never done it this early in a relationship. I assumed that it was a good sign, he was calling whatever this was a 'relationship.'

I wondered how long it had been since his last fling and then I wondered how long it was before they jumped into the sack.

I could almost guarantee I was the only woman who wouldn't just roll over and give him what he wanted.

Although, he was behaving like a gentleman. Could this guy really be this nice? I doubt it.

He still has his game face on. Maybe this is the way he seduces everyone. He pretends to be nice and he doesn't push, so then his prey would surmise that he's a gentleman. Then they realize, they'll have to seduce *him*. After all, he's not aggressive. He must be a nice guy, right?

My mind wandered to all those articles I had read about him. How he was such a womanizer and how he had such a bad temper. I hadn't seen that side of him. But, then again, I haven't done anything to make him really angry yet.

Maybe telling him I wasn't going to have sex with him – ever, maybe that would make him angry. Well, I wasn't about to tell him tonight.

I'm sure he'd laugh and not believe me anyway. People always have a hard time believing it. I still had a difficult time believing it myself!

I was impressed though, I could tell he put a lot of time into the meal and setting the table. Dinner was ready, so he pulled the chair out for me. I sat down and put the napkin in my lap.

He came behind me with a plate. It looked like something from one of my favorite Naples restaurants. He sat down and watched as I cut a bite of chicken. It looked really good, and smelled fantastic.

"My cooking is so good, you're going to have a culinary orgasm," he said.

I raised my eyebrows. "I've never heard that expression before."

"I just meant this is the best meal I make."

"I'm not a prude – it's maybe not a word for the dinner

table, you know?" I said with the chicken hovering on my fork.

"Yeah, definitely, you're right. Well?" he said, waiting impatiently for the verdict.

I took that first bite. It was really good.

"Excellent, Mark." I winked at him.

When we finished up dinner, I helped him clear the table. "You really are good in the kitchen," I said.

"Wait until you see me in the..." he stopped. I shook my head disapprovingly. "Right, we're taking it slow. I don't mean to be so aggressive," he said. I exhaled. "Did I offend you?" he asked.

"No," I said quietly.

"I'm sorry, Megan. It's just, you're so beautiful and it's so quick, but I'm totally falling for you. I find myself thinking about you all the time, and honestly, I feel like I've known you a very long time." And then he pushed me against the counter and kissed me.

I pushed him off after a minute. "I need to say something to you." I took his hand and walked him to the living room and sat on the couch. I grabbed his hands and faced him.

"What is it?" he asked.

I paused for a few seconds to think about what I was going to say. "All right Mark, this is the thing. I'm going to be the love of your *life*. This is a once in a lifetime thing, the kind of thing you only hear about in legends. People our age don't have romances like this anymore. You will love me so deeply; you will physically ache for me."

He looked at me like he was dizzy and he was kind of smiling in disbelief. "If you want me, if you want *this*, it has to be on my terms."

I cupped my hands around his face. "Now, I'm not the kind of woman you just want to jump into bed with, right?" I asked sincerely.

"No, of course not," he said smiling. Then he thought about it. "Wait, yes, yes, you are." He kissed me, hard. "I'm really turned on right now," he said.

"Uh oh." I stood up. "I think we'd better call it a night." I grabbed my purse and walked toward the door, digging for my keys. "Aren't you going to walk me to my car?" I asked. He looked down.

He came over to me a minute later. "Please don't leave. I'm not used to waiting, but I don't want you to go. No one has ever said stuff like that to me before, and I totally believe it. Please, we'll just watch TV or something. I will keep my hands to myself, I promise."

He turned the television on.

"What do you want to watch?" I asked.

"I really don't want to watch TV right now," he said with a smile.

"Well, we're not going to be doing any more kissing tonight, Tiger, or I'll have to pry you off with a crowbar," I said.

We did a search for movies and found a classic we both agreed on. We managed to watch TV for about an hour but he kept touching me.

Believe me, I didn't mind, but it made me nervous. Could I stop myself with Mark?

"I'm going to go home now," I said.

"Okay, it's time for my cold shower, anyway." He stood up and pulled me to my feet. "Come on, I'll walk you to your car. I have tomorrow off. Do you want to see me?"

"Definitely," I said. We walked out to the car and he

opened my door, then put his arms around my waist and gazed down into my eyes.

"What?" I asked. He looked like he really wanted to say something.

He was hesitant. "I think you *are* the love of my life, Megan," he said. He sounded surprised.

I said matter-of-factly, "I know."

He stood there a long time with his arms around me. It was very innocent...and weird. He gave me a kiss and I drove home thinking how crazy it was that Mark Taylor was my boyfriend. He wasn't exactly the poster boy for celibacy.

CHAPTER 7

Weeks went by and I found myself thinking and fantasizing about Mark all day. This was turning into something unexpected. I was completely in love with this guy. He was everything I wanted. I didn't see that coming.

About a month into the relationship, Mark came over to have dinner at my place. I made Chicken Cordon Bleu, baby potatoes and green beans. He had a few bites and then said, "I can see why they say 'a way to a man's heart is through his stomach.'"

And without thinking I blurted out, "And all these years, you thought it was through your pants." He laughed and my eyes widened. "Sorry, I don't think before I speak."

We finished the meal and he helped me clean up afterwards. Not wanting to risk either of us getting frisky, I suggested we play Monopoly.

"You want to play Monopoly?"

I nodded. He laughed.

"Well, I can honestly say, that's one thing I've never done on a date."

He looked at all the properties and then laughed. "What?" I asked.

He pointed down to the board. "Some of these are your real properties."

I smiled. "Yeah, all of them are. I had a Monopoly Board custom made with all the properties I own." He looked at me like I was crazy.

"What?" I asked innocently.

"I wonder why you think some of the stuff you do is normal."

"What do you mean?"

"Don't take this the wrong way, but you're a little pretentious. I mean, Megan, this is kind of ridiculous." And then it struck me.

I looked at him with sincerity and said, "I'm obnoxious."

"Yeah." He nodded and agreed.

"Wow. No one has ever pointed that out to me. How long have I been like this?"

"I can't be sure, but at least a few weeks!"

Mark twisted in his chair and grunted. "What's the matter?" I asked him.

"My back!" he said as he sat down on the floor in front of me. He said the director had him riding a horse for hours for a scene and he was sore. I told him to take his shirt off and I would rub his back. No big deal – I'm a big girl; I figured I could handle it. Then he took his shirt off and my little piggies froze into fists. I sat up real straight. This was going to be painful.

I looked up at the ceiling. I don't know what I thought I was going to see when I looked up. I slowly put my hands on his shoulders and closed my eyes. His skin felt so warm, and he made little noises that sent shivers up my spine. I just kept repeating to myself, 'It's only a backrub, it's only a backrub.' I thought I would be okay as long as he stayed with his back to me.

That was the moment he decided to turn around. I heard a voice tell me 'incoming pecs, twelve o'clock,' and I tried not to make eye contact. I couldn't look directly at them. I didn't want to burn my retinas. Then he came in for the kill. The man must know my weakness. I must be strong…can't look. And then he kissed me. What harm is there in kissing, really?

Oh, there it is, there's the harm. I pushed him back. "It's getting late," I said.

He smiled a little crookedly and put his shirt on. "If I didn't know better, I'd think you can't control yourself."

I giggled nervously. "I can't. You…you need to go." I gave him a peck on the cheek. He told me he would call and then he left.

★ ★ ★ ★ ★

I went to work the next day and told Carol about the Monopoly board and asked her if she thought I was pretentious.

"Megan, you went out and spent a thousand dollars on a Lacoste tennis wardrobe to play Wii."

"So, that's a yes?" I asked, and I knew from her dirty look that it was. I told her I'd given him a backrub without his shirt and he was perfect. I did not tell her I had to send him home because I was afraid of what could happen, I just said we should not be spending so much time at my house.

The next night was more of the same, kissing and potential danger! We watched television, on separate couches. I fell asleep. I woke up to Mark's voice, but when I looked over at him, he'd fallen asleep too. Disoriented, I finally realized one of his movies was on. He was shooting at someone. I didn't know what movie it was. I typed in 'Mark Taylor' on the search mode on my television. *The E! Hollywood Story of Mark Taylor* was coming on, so I set it to record. He *was* my boyfriend. I thought I should watch it.

It was weird watching him on television and then looking at him on the sofa. He was even better looking in person, but he was hot in High-Definition, too. I checked the time on the television – it was 4:00 am. I decided not to wake him though I knew it wouldn't look good if anyone saw him leaving my house in the morning. But I knew he was exhausted and I didn't want him driving at four in the morning. I went into my bedroom and went back to sleep.

I woke a few hours later to the smell of bacon and the sound of laughter. I jumped out of bed and practically flew into the kitchen. There was Mark, standing with my housekeeper Maria, eating bacon.

"Good morning, Ms. Megan," Maria said with a scowl.

"Good morning, Maria," I said.

Mark came over and kissed me. "Good morning, baby," he said.

"Good morning." I smiled at him and wrinkled my nose at Maria when she gave me 'the look' of disapproval.

"You didn't tell me you were having Mr. Taylor spend the night. I would've prepared the guest room."

"Well, I didn't know he was spending the night. We both fell asleep watching television." I got defensive. "Nothing inappropriate happened. I slept in my bed…alone!"

Mark came over to me with breakfast plates for the both of us and whispered, "Why are you defending yourself to the help?" I just smiled at him and then gave Maria a dirty look. She gave me one right back.

Mark scarfed down his food and then left. He had to go home since he didn't have a change of clothes at the house. It was Sunday and he said he was going to church with me. He kissed me and said goodbye to Maria and then left. I went into the kitchen, where Maria was cleaning up. "You know," she said, "he really shouldn't be spending the night. People are going to get the wrong idea."

"Well, you know what, Maria? They get the wrong idea anyway. We're both adults."

"Have you told him yet?"

"No. I know what's going to happen."

"I don't know. This one is different."

"C'mon. You only spent a few minutes with him."

"This is true, but I see the way he looks at you. He cares about you already."

I wasn't buying it. This perfect guy is going to bolt when I tell him. "I have to go get ready for church."

"He's going to church with you? Sounds serious to me."

"We'll see."

Sitting in church, I could feel Mark staring at me as I looked at the stage, waiting for the service to begin. "I don't get the whole church thing. How can you not do all the stuff you used to?"

"I hear voices."

He looked at me like I was insane.

"I realize that makes me sound crazy."

"It sure does...and you said *voices*. Like, there's more than one?"

"You've never had a voice in your head tell you not to do something? Or, a voice tells you *to* do something?"

"Yeah. But I thought that was, like, a conscience."

"Well, last night, I had one voice in my head telling me to kick you out and say goodnight. And I had another voice tell me to take you into the bedroom. If I had listened to that voice, we wouldn't be in church right now." He raised an eyebrow and grinned at me. "Every time I look at you, I have to repent," I said.

Mark said, "I feel like everyone is staring at us."

"Believe me, 'The Lottery Heiress' attending church with 'The Sexiest Man Alive' is stare-worthy," I said.

He squirmed in his seat. "It makes me uncomfortable."

"I've never brought a man to church with me before. It may be *me* they're staring at. And then *you're* the one I bring. They'll probably lay hands on me after the service."

"I haven't ever gone to church with anyone before. This may shock you, but the women I date aren't big church goers," he said.

"Wow. That *is* surprising," I said sarcastically as I smacked him on the thigh.

The pastor and his wife came up to us and shook Mark's hand. Other church members came to be introduced, and once the service started, Mark got more comfortable. No one made a big deal about him being a celebrity. No one mentioned his movies or television series. They just treated him like everyone else.

★ ★ ★ ★ ★

The next night, I met him at his house. It was very late because he'd been working late on the set. We had already eaten dinner and decided to just hang out at the house since he had to be up early again the next morning.

I was in the kitchen fixing us snacks and drinks. He started surfing through the channels. "Hey," he called out, "one of my movies is on."

"Oh, I'll be right there." I came out with a tray, picked up my drink and sat back, right next to him on the couch. He had his legs on the ottoman. The remote was on his left thigh. He had one arm around me and held his drink in the other hand.

"Oh, this is a good part. I haven't seen this movie since the premiere."

"You don't watch yourself when your movies come on television?"

"I don't know any actor who does."

It was a chase scene with a car and motorcycle. Mark was driving the motorcycle and shooting at the car in front of him. "Which movie is this?" I asked.

"Don O'Malley."

Oh great. This movie barely managed an R-rating. I wouldn't normally watch it but it did have my boyfriend in it.

"I did all my own stunts in this." The car swerved and hit a bridge abutment. Mark pulled a woman out of the back seat. The 'bad guys' were dead. He put her on his motorcycle and they took off.

"See that black eye? That's not make-up. My ex-girlfriend clocked me on the set."

"She sounds like a nice girl. I can't imagine why

you're not with her anymore."

He kissed me. "She was nothing like you. No one is." The kissing escalated. I found myself going right along too. Then I forced myself to stop leading him on, when I knew in my heart he was going to leave. Oh, I wanted him to stay. I wanted him to stay and do things to me that haven't been done to me in a very long time.

I exhaled, pushing the air forcefully between my lips. "There's something I need to tell you."

He paused the television. "What is it?"

"I wanted to remind you that I'm really old-fashioned."

"Believe me, I *know*."

"I just really want to take it slow, Mark."

"Megan, it's been a month – If we were moving any *slower*, I'd have to have my balls amputated."

"I'm sorry..." I said as I put my hands over my face and laughed.

"I've been more than patient. I think you know by now I'm not going anywhere."

He resumed the movie. His character was alone with the girl he had rescued in a house somewhere. He took his shirt off and started kissing the actress while he undressed her.

"This doesn't bother you to watch this?" I asked him.

"No, why? It's just a movie."

"Here I am sitting with you, and you're that person on TV. It's weird."

"Is this making you uncomfortable to watch me with someone else?"

"Honestly, yeah. I don't know why. I mean, I didn't even know you then."

"Yes, you did. This movie was released six years ago."

"I didn't know you. You were just a guy lying on the floor," I said as I touched the side of his face. I returned my attention to the TV.

"Oh yeah, this is pretty heavy content. Are you upset?"

"No, I'm jealous." He laughed. I put my hand over my mouth and looked away.

"Why don't you tell me when this part is over?"

"Why don't I just kiss you 'til it's over?"

Sarcastically I said, "Yeah, that's a good idea." He kissed me, one long, slow kiss.

"The rest of the movie isn't bad. You shouldn't have to cover your eyes again."

"Isn't this girl coming back?"

"No, I wind up shooting her."

I laughed. "I'm not looking forward to our break up."

"I don't plan on breaking up with you!"

His phone rang and he pulled it out of his pocket. "Sorry, I have to take this, it's my agent." He went into the other room. I was pretty engrossed in this movie, probably because the star was walking around in my living room. It was very strange – cool, but strange.

Sometimes when you meet celebrities, they are shorter in person, or less attractive, but Mark was tall and even better looking. And in person, he has his shirt on, thank God, because he was barely dressed in this scene!

Mark came back and looked troubled. He put his phone on the table. "My agent wants me to take a role I'm not sure about."

"What's the problem?"

"It's a re-make of *Gone with the Wind*."

"No, say it isn't so!"

"They're offering me ten million dollars. That's more than I've ever made on one film."

"I'll give you ten million *not* to do it."

"My manager's pushing me too. I've read the script. I'm not thrilled."

"Who do they want you to play?"

"Rhett Butler."

"Oh, well then you get to deliver that classic line. 'Frankly, my dear…'"

"Yeah, except now Rhett says the 'F' word." Mark picked up a pretzel. "What do you think?"

"Go with your gut."

"Yeah, I think you're right. I mean, who wants to watch *Gone with the Wind* in 3-D?"

He sat down, pointing at the TV. "Oh look, this is the best part." Mark's character was shooting a bunch of people. I watched Mark laughing at the movie. I could tell he really loved being an actor.

What was I going to do with this guy? Well, I knew what I'd like to do. Look at that smile! It wouldn't last long after I told him about the sex thing. Too bad – I like this one so much. He is just too cute. He understands my jokes and likes to tell me I'm pretty. Oh well, we'd had a good run. Mark turned to me and pulled me on his lap. He kissed me and I could feel his hands creeping up the back of my shirt. He tried to unsnap my bra and I knew I had better stop it now!

Dear God, I was in big trouble. We were both breathing heavy and I was losing willpower.

He whispered, "I want to make love to you," as he kissed my neck and stuck his tongue in my ear.

"I can tell. We need to stop," I said. I could hardly get my mouth to work; all it wanted to do was kiss him some more.

"C'mon, Megan. It's been a month. You're *killing*

me."

"There's something I need to tell you, Mark. There's something I've been hiding from you."

He got serious and backed up. "Please don't say it's a penis."

I laughed, and relaxed a little bit. "No, we're all good down there. Look, I know I should've told you this, probably weeks ago, but I like you and I didn't think you'd stick around..."

He pulled away a little bit more, concerned. "What is it?"

"I don't know how to tell you this."

He turned his whole body towards me and looked very serious. "Are you married?"

"I wish!"

"Megan, just tell me!"

Finally I looked him straight in the eye and said, as fast as I could, "I'm-not-having-sex-until-I-get-married." I exhaled really fast.

He cracked up. He sounded a little hysterical. "What was that?"

"Sorry. I'm not having sex until I'm married." The man honestly looked horrified. "I live my life according to the Bible, which means no sex outside of marriage."

"You can't have sex 'til you're married?" He crossed his arms and tilted his head.

"Yeah, I'm sorry, it's just... it's been a month and you're still here and we haven't had sex, I kind of thought you figured it out. I mean, we've been going to church together and everything." I felt bad. I said, "I'm sorry. It was selfish. I should've told you." Then I got defensive. "You know, if this were thirty years ago, we wouldn't even need to be having this conversation."

He sat back on the couch and looked at me in disbelief. I stood up and said, "Well, it was nice meeting you." I stuck out my hand. He stared at it, then back at my face.

"What are you doing?"

"I'm saying goodbye," I said. "You're not getting any, so this is when you get up and go."

He smirked and gave me a nod. "Sit down." He sat forward and clasped his hands between his knees. "Honestly, if you had told me this a month ago, it would've been over. Unfortunately for me, I have feelings for you now." He looked down. Then he said something I was not prepared to hear. "I'm in *love* with you."

"But, you *know* me!"

He smiled shyly. "Clearly, not as well as I'd like to."

I was in total disbelief. "You're not dumping me?"

"Absolutely not. So you're a virgin – big deal."

"Yeah, about that…not so much."

"So, you've had sex before?"

I explained to him what happened at the hospital and how I went to church and decided to wait until I get married to have sex. He reacted, well, better than I expected.

"Do you know how many women throw themselves at me?"

"No. And I don't want to."

"Megan, women come up to me all the time and want to have sex with me. I mean – complete strangers. I can't see myself being serious about someone who sleeps with me right away because then I think she must hop right into bed with *everyone*." He touched my face. "But you're different. You're special. You're still *dressed*."

I took his hand and held it in my lap, squeezed it tight.

"How can you be for real?"

"What can I say? I'm a dream come true."

I shook my head. "Out of all the guys in the world, Mark Taylor is the one that stays!"

He kissed me. "Do you love me, Megan?"

"I knew I loved you the first night at dinner."

"So...we love each other."

"Yup."

"And, we can't have sex?"

"Nope."

There was an uncomfortable silence. We looked anywhere but at each other. I took a sip of my tea. "But we can talk," I said.

He paused. "Can we have oral sex?"

I wasn't expecting that. I crossed my legs and leaned in. "Only if you mean *talking* about it."

"Heavy petting?" he asked.

"Hey, this isn't the zoo."

He shoved a hand through his hair and he said it was a new experience for him. I told him it was for me too, since everyone normally leaves when I tell them. He was worried I could give sex up easily – maybe I didn't enjoy it. I reassured him I enjoyed sex and wanted to have it again – as soon as possible.

I explained to him that cutting sex out of my life was like when I had to cut sugar out of my diet. Once it was gone, I didn't miss it much. Unfortunately, like sugar, once I got a taste of a man, I couldn't stop myself. Enter Mark Taylor. Sugar! Sugar! Sugar!

He still didn't fully understand it and I was having trouble understanding it too. I had an international sex symbol on my couch and I couldn't jump his bones. I explained that after my coma, I knew I had to make some changes in my life. The first one was trying to have higher standards than my own.

He asked again, "So, you won't have sex with me?"

"Not unless we're married."

"How long has it been?"

"I haven't had sex in years."

"Years?!"

"Yeah, before Rick."

"You didn't even have sex with your fiancé?"

"Nope."

"Wow."

"Well, it was a lot easier when I was dating unattractive guys. It's not so easy with 'The Sexiest Man Alive.'"

"Oh, I get it now; you were dating people you weren't attracted to, on purpose."

"I mean, I want you, Mark. More than I've ever wanted anyone."

"Trust me, you're only punishing yourself! Come here. I want to show you what I did." He took my hand and led me to the bedroom, where he had scattered hundreds of red rose petals all over the bed and floor. I was supposed to be amazed, I guess, but I am, after all, me. So I said the first thing I thought of.

"Wow. What a mess. Who's going to clean *that* up?"

And he laughed. "Megan, do you remember when you said you're hard to love?"

"Yeah," I said, drooping. I totally believed it.

"Well, it's not hard for me," he said. "I love you like – I don't know – something crazy." He gave me a quick, hard kiss.

"So, tonight was supposed to be *the night*, huh?"

He nodded.

"I'm sorry. I'm not a very romantic person. I mean, this is very nice, but I don't need all this," I said, pointing to the rose petals.

★ ★ ★ ★ ★

As the weeks went by, I could feel my self-control diminishing quickly. Every time he touched me, my mind raced to the bedroom. I decided since I didn't fully trust either one of us, we shouldn't spend so much time at our houses. We started going out to do things.

We went to the late-late movies to avoid the crowds. We also took long walks on the beach and when we wanted to get away, we'd fly out to Captiva or drive to Naples.

For the next couple of months, Mark spent every moment he wasn't working with me. We were in deep and we both knew it. We were taking more and more trips to avoid doing something we shouldn't. We would take day trips to major cities and visit museums and gourmet restaurants. We even flew into the Sebring Raceway and raced cars around the track. And Mark almost caught up to me a few times.

I still couldn't believe I was dating Mark Taylor. He was so different from the way the media portrayed him. This ladies' man was in a relationship where he not only was faithful, but was not having sex. I had dated many untrustworthy people. I can't recall how many guys I dated said they were faithful, when all they wanted was my money. As a result, I have trust issues. With Mark, all those walls I built up just came tumbling down.

He was the outdoorsy type, so he made me try hiking and climbing. I don't like heights, but I was trying to be open-minded since those things were important to him.

He even made me try parasailing. I wouldn't do that again. I swear I saw fins in the water. Mark said it was my imagination, but I have 20/20 vision – and he does not! When I wasn't with him, my mind wandered, sometimes to very inappropriate places. It was difficult for me to watch his movies and not wish I was the woman he was with. I wondered what kind of lover he was. There was no insight from his movies. He was ravenous in *Don O'Malley* and gentle in *You're the One*. I was curious, but that's not a question you ask a guy you're trying to avoid having sex with.

Naples was one of Mark's favorite places. We were always surrounded by celebrities. It wasn't a big deal walking around with the common folk – except these common folk are made up of more millionaires, per capita, than other city in Florida.

Don't get me wrong, of course we traveled with my security. Mark and I liked eating and shopping on 5th Avenue. It was really fun shopping with him there, since he was a millionaire too.

Even though I had more money than him, it wasn't weird. I guess it because he was famous. He was way more recognizable than me. When I was with Mark, the attention was on him. That was really nice for a change. I liked being in his shadow. It felt comfortable. And I think he liked the fact that I sincerely didn't want or need the money or fame.

When we did risk a night in, we'd watch movies at my house. He taught me how to critique movies and he told me what all those weird titles and names meant at the closing credits.

He made me watch some great movies I had never seen, like *Cool Hand Luke*, *The Shawshank Redemption* and *Citizen Kane*. I made him watch some very bad comedies. I laughed way more than he did, and then he made me watch more of his movies.

I tried to convince him that I do see serious movies on occasion. I would just rather watch something funny, even if it is stupid. Like in real life, I would rather laugh than cry. I have cried enough.

I wondered how much longer Mark would hold out. I didn't want to keep sending him home. I wanted to start sending him to my bedroom.

I hoped he would realize this thing we had was worth waiting for, but I knew it had to be tough for a guy like him. He was gorgeous, and rich and famous. Why *wasn't* I having sex with this guy?

I could not believe my self-control. It was beyond belief. If I had met him when we were both still drinking, that would've been scary. That would have been a rocky ride – so to speak. Oh well, I know everything happens for a reason, but I wanted him and I didn't know how much more I could stand. He was the epitome of what a man should be. I felt so deprived. So starved. God help me.

One night while Mark and I were out, Cindy called and said she was doing a gig at a comedy club the next night. Mark was free to come with me, so we packed overnight bags and then we made the drive to Miami. We took my Range Rover and I let Mark drive. I called Cindy and told her we were in town, and then I showed him the neighborhood where I used to live and the night clubs I used to frequent. He showed me where he got arrested for disorderly conduct. Then he showed me where he got pulled over and arrested for a DUI.

Mark and I decided to go to his house before we had dinner. We parked the Range Rover in the driveway. When we got to the front door, I was reminded instantly of why I loved this place. He led me through the house, showing me all of the things he'd done to the house since I was there last. We went into his bedroom so I could see how it was remodeled.

"You know, I took a shower in there?" I said, as I pointed to the bathroom.

"If you play your cards right this weekend, we can make that happen again!"

I put my hand on his chest, "Don't get yourself worked up, Mark." He kissed me, very hard. He pointed to the bed.

"That's a new mattress. You want to try it out?"

"Awe, did you wear out the last one?"

He pulled me close and kissed me. "You're the only woman I've ever brought here."

I was skeptical. "Seriously?"

"Seriously, Megan. You're the only one."

"Oh," I said with surprise.

"You know what's weird? I stayed here right before I went to Fort Myers."

"Why were you in Miami?"

"I shot a pilot for television."

"Why would you do a TV series? I thought movie actors were more respected."

"There are a lot of movie stars doing television now. You just have to get the right series. There are big names directing and producing television now."

"So, would you take it if the show gets picked up?"

"That depends. Can you give me a reason to stay?"

"I think I could give you several." I kissed him. Sometimes I *hate* being good. He kissed me again and told me he wanted to change for dinner. I threw my bag on a chair since the bed wasn't made yet. I ran my hand down one of the tall mahogany bedposts. The room had a fireplace and a beautiful dark hardwood floor and trim.

There wasn't much furniture, but enough to get by for one night. In fact, the whole house was relatively unfurnished considering he had owned it for seven years. I wondered if he would ever make this house a home. I wondered what would happen if he got the show.

I went out to the kitchen, where Mark was pouring us some drinks. I walked up to the counter where he was and he grabbed me and put his arms around me.

"You wanna get a bite now?"

He smiled, "Sure, but make it quick, I'm ready for dinner!"

"You're naughty!"

Mark said he wanted to take his car. I didn't mind, I haven't driven in this area in a while anyway. Plus, I like a man to be in control. You can tell a lot about a guy by the way he drives. As we walked towards the garage, I asked what kind of car he had.

"Mercedes."

"Oh," I said disappointed.

"Not a fan?"

"I just prefer Audi or BMW."

"Oh, I think you'll like *my* car," he said, then opened the garage door to reveal a Mercedes-Benz McLaren SLR Roadster.

In case you don't know, that was a very cool, very expensive car! It had gull wings that went forward and up. That was a car for the ultra-rich.

He grabbed the keys and went to unlock the doors, while I goggled at the car. I grinned. "That's not just a Mercedes. It's a McLaren! What year is this?"

Mark could tell I was getting excited. "It's a 2007."

"This is the only Mercedes I ever wanted! I should've bought one while they were still in production."

He unlocked the car and lifted my door for me. I watched it go up towards the ceiling.

"I know it's wrong to say, but I'm aroused right now," I said as I got into the sleek, black car.

He looked at me to see if I was serious. I wasn't laughing. Mark pulled my door down. He walked around the car and got in, closed his own door. I ran my hand over the red leather interior. The seats were like butter. I kissed him. "I already loved you, but now I love you *even* more." He laughed.

I liked watching him shift the car. I was seriously turned on. That car was fast. There were over six hundred horses under the hood and he was commanding every one of them. The veins on his right hand and arm were popping out. He looked at me.

"Are you okay, babe?" He said as he tapped my left leg.

"Oh yeah – I'm just listening to the engine."

"Do you want to drive home?"

"No. I like watching you drive."

Mark laughed. "You are turned on, aren't you?"

"I think that's why you *bought* this car, Mark." I said as I squeezed his leg.

We went to a very trendy steak restaurant in South Beach. The paparazzi were snapping our pictures left and right. It didn't help that we showed up in the McLaren. We were seated in the front tables in the windows of the restaurant.

Mark said that was done on purpose so everyone could see this restaurant served rich and famous patrons. There were fans pushing each other against the glass to get a look and that's as close as they were going to get. The prices definitely kept the average person out! We left the restaurant and headed back to Mark's house. It was getting late. We pulled the car into the garage. We walked into the house and grabbed a couple of drinks and then decided to go to bed.

A few minutes went by, and I changed into my pajamas and put my iPod on. I was taking my clothes out of the bag so they wouldn't be all wrinkled the next day. He came up behind me and scared me because I didn't hear him. "Here are the sheets," he said.

"Argh!" I jumped back.

"Sorry, Megan." He went to the opposite side of the bed. "Do you want to grab that side?" He flung the sheet across the mattress. I grabbed the other side and helped tuck it in. He threw the top sheet out and tossed a blanket onto the bed. We put on the pillowcases. "I thought maybe we could talk some more or watch some television or something."

"I think we'd better just call it a night. I don't think there should be any more kissing…" Just as I said that, he pulled me against him and kissed me. It felt so good. Oh, Lord, give me strength. I pushed him away gently. "Go to bed, Mark."

He let me go. "I love you."

"Love you too, Mark." I blew him a kiss. He smiled. Poor guy, he looked as frustrated as I was. I was lying in bed watching the big rattan ceiling fan spin. I seriously contemplated going into Mark's bedroom and pouncing on him. I wondered if I was building up how incredible it would be. I have been thinking about what this guy would be like in bed since our first date. What if I crept into his room and seduced him, and it didn't live up to my expectations?

I mean, if I'm going to be *damned*, I'd better see fireworks – that's all I'm saying. I decided to stick to my guns and do the right thing and not have sex with 'The Sexiest Man Alive.' I just went to sleep alone. What a shame when Mark Taylor is right down the hall.

I woke up the next morning and hopped right into the shower. When I got dressed, Mark was cooking eggs and bacon and the smell alone made my stomach growl. I decided to just clip my hair and do my make-up after breakfast. I walked out and said, "Good morning." I started walking over to the kitchen but stopped, staring down at the floor.

"What are you looking at?" he asked.

"Nothing. It's just, that's the first place I ever saw you." I walked over to the spot where I had found him.

"I don't really want to remember that," he said as he came up behind me.

"Well, I will never forget, Mark. I could've lost you on that day and where would I be right now?" He walked over to me and put his arms around me. Funny how I forced myself to receive hugs from anyone else, but his made me feel so good.

We walked back into the kitchen, hand in hand. He poured us both some coffee.

"Thanks," I said. Mark set a plate in front of me and I

dug in. "I can't wait to see Cindy's set!"

"I hope she's funny," he said.

"She is. Do you think I would hang out with someone who wasn't funny?"

He laughed. "No way!"

We took the McLaren again, and spent the day shopping and sight-seeing. I was never bored with this guy. He knew how to have fun even during mundane activities. We ate lunch at a posh restaurant and were surrounded by fans.

Miami was not as calm as Fort Myers or Captiva when it came to celebrity sightings. Mark and I actually got separated for a little while when he got rushed outside of a store. I was sorry I hadn't called my security team and made them come with us. I let my guard down and was regretful about it.

Cindy called and asked us to meet her at 'The Joke Factory' in Miami. She saved a table for us right in front. As soon as we walked over to the table, she hugged me. When she hugged Mark, she said, "I'm glad she didn't give you the 'Hooters Kiss of Death' before I got to meet you!" We sat down.

"The what?" he asked with a chuckle.

I smirked at her and shook my head.

"You mean you didn't tell him?"

"No, I didn't, Cindy."

The waitress came over to get our drink order. She gave Mark a huge smile and then left.

"When Megan wants to break up with someone, she takes them to Hooters and then dumps them!"

Mark laughed. "Megan, is that true?"

I just looked at him and gave him a mischievous smile.

She kept staring at Mark, and giggling. Even worse,

she kept moving closer and closer to him, hitting him flirtatiously every time he said anything even remotely charming. It was ridiculous. Mark was used to it, but I wasn't used to my friends acting so weird around a celebrity, especially since she had met other celebrities with me before.

"Jeff Lemieux is headlining, huh?" I asked.

"Yeah, can you believe that jerk is back in Miami?" she said.

I shrugged. "Couldn't make it in L.A.?"

"Mark, do you know the best comedian I ever saw?" She pointed at me. "This one right here," she said.

He looked at me in surprise. "You never told me you did stand-up."

I shrugged my shoulders, took a sip of my drink and looked around. "It's not a big deal."

"Don't believe that, Mark," Cindy said. "When her name was on the marquee, it was standing room only."

I looked at Mark. "It was also dollar draft night." Mark laughed.

"That's not true either. No dollar drafts on Saturday, Megan."

"How come you quit?" Mark asked me.

Cindy butted in. "Phillip didn't like it."

"You know, you act like he controlled my whole life," I said to Cindy.

"He did. Phillip was *not* a very nice person, Mark," she said.

"Oh, I wish I could've heard your act," Mark said.

"Yeah? Well, I was a lot funnier before my parents' accident. *That's* why I stopped doing stand-up. I didn't feel funny anymore."

"Well, Megan, you should at least listen to your friend

and write a book," Cindy said.

"What book?" asked Mark.

"Cindy wants me to write a book based on my life," I said, swirling my tea around in the glass. "I can't imagine what I would write about."

"You could write about loss and coping. And you could do it in a funny way that would help people," she said.

"And what would I call it? The Lottery Heiress?"

Mark looked at the two of us laughing our heads off. "You know Megan, that's not a bad idea." Then he excused himself and went to the restroom.

"How come Mark didn't know you were a stand-up?" she asked.

"Unlike you, I don't feel the need to tell everyone every detail about my life."

"Megan, it's time you let someone get to know you," she said.

"Mark knows me – probably better than any man ever did. Some part of me is still waiting for this thing to go wrong. I can't help feel that maybe there's a chance I'm going to lose him, too. And honestly, I don't think I can through that ever again."

"Listen, no risk – no reward, who taught me that?"

I got annoyed. I knew she was right. "*I did.*" I rolled my eyes.

"Right! I have to go; I'm on after this clown." She headed toward the stage. Mark came back to the table and kissed me.

Cindy performed her set and got lots of laughs. After the show, the three of us went to a Cuban restaurant to grab something to eat. I was a little disappointed her husband didn't show up. Even if he didn't like her doing stand-up, I thought he should at least be there to support her. We talked for a couple of hours and then Cindy drove home.

"How come you didn't tell me you wanted to be a stand-up comedian?"

"Because when I tell people, they want me to be funny all the time."

"But you *are* funny," he said.

"I know, but I don't like being under pressure to be funny. Plus, I never got over the whole stalking thing. It was always in the back of my mind."

"I can understand that. I've had my share of obsessed fans."

The other side of the restaurant had a dance club. It was very loud.

"Do you want to go over and check out the club?" Mark asked me.

"But they have Latin dancing there," I said. For some reason, this amused him.

"C'mon, let's go do a little salsa-ing," he said with a cocky smile.

"Oh, thanks, but I think that's the 'forbidden dance.'"

"No, that's the Lambada."

"Mark, I can't dance," I confessed.

"It's okay. Didn't you see my movie *Hot Latin Nights*? I played a young Cuban who falls in love with a white girl who can't dance." He got out of the booth and put his hand out to pull me up. "Trust me; I had months of lessons for that movie. I can teach anyone to dance."

"You are about to see some real comedy, my friend." We went next door to the nightclub. Mark had no idea what he was in for.

CHAPTER 8

The smell of cologne and desperation filled the air. We proceeded to the dance floor, where he stood and crossed his arms. "Show me your best moves," he said.

I laughed nervously and just stood there, hoping he'd let me off the hook but he insisted. "C'mon, Megan, do your thing." I danced the only way I knew how – not well.

Before I knew it, he started laughing so hard his face turned red. "You know, Megan; you really shouldn't dance without a helmet – you could really hurt yourself!"

"I told you I couldn't dance." That's why I used to drink and make fun of everyone else dancing. Very few people knew I couldn't dance. I had convinced them I just liked drinking better.

"You have no rhythm," he said.

"Well, I can't *dance*. Who cares?"

"I will, if someone sends pictures of me and you to *US Weekly*."

Many of the patrons recognized him, but they didn't bother him. They just watched him try and teach the gringa some dance moves. It was quite a spectacle.

Without knowing it, we re-enacted much of the dance scenes from his movie. I heard many of the people in the club speaking Spanish and saying *Hot Latin Nights* in English. There was also laughter, so I assumed I was just as bad as the white girl in the movie.

A few songs in, I thought I was getting better. But Mark said, "Wow, you're really terrible."

"Thanks, honey," I said.

He laughed. "I mean, you warned me, but wow, you were right."

"Maybe you're just not a good teacher," I said with a smile.

"No, you're really terrible." Then he gave me a kiss, which took some of the sting from his words... The music was so loud. It felt like my heart was beating out of my chest. We were getting hot, so we decided to get a drink at the bar.

Mark asked for a mineral water and I asked for a virgin 'Miami Vice,' which is a Piña Colada and Strawberry Daiquiri combined. It was huge. It tasted good – weird, but good. They said it wasn't from a mix, but I couldn't really distinguish the tastes.

I drank it quickly and we headed back out to the dance floor. The music slowed down and Mark pulled me in very close. He was moving his hands slowly down my sides and then turned me around. He pulled me in close again and we swayed with the music.

It was getting very hot in there. I knew I was going to a point of no return when he was sweating all over me and I didn't even want to use sanitizer. He put his hands on my hips and started moving me in ways I knew were not appropriate for a church girl. But I went right along with it. I felt a little like everything was going in slow motion. Something was not right.

There was a battle raging in my mind. I asked myself what the big deal was. We were just dancing. It wasn't like we were naked. It was *just* dancing. But, I did want him desperately.

And that's when he twirled me around, and with one hand wrapped around my back and one on my thigh, he started grinding on me. And I just let him. I knew I was setting myself up for more trouble. Lord knows how I love trouble.

He kissed me and I kissed him right back. I couldn't dance the right way, but grinding on Mark came naturally somehow. I looked around and everyone else was doing the same thing. Everyone was dancing way too close.

There was not enough room between Mark and me to even exhale. And then someone came up and started taking pictures with a heavy flash. Mark grabbed my hand and we squeezed through the crowd to the exit.

We got back in the McLaren and headed to his house. He put his hand on my knee between shifting. "Are you all right, Megan?"

"Yeah. I think it was time for us to go, anyway."

"Yeah, you're probably right."

"I... I think there was alcohol in that drink. I don't feel right."

"Do I need to pull over? No puking in the McLaren!"

"I'm not going to be sick, but I'm definitely buzzed."

"Huh. So, that's why you seem like you let your inhibitions down a little."

"What do you mean?"

"You know, the way we were dancing."

"I want you. I mean – it's taking everything I have not to have sex with you." We didn't say much more to each other after that so I thought we took it a little too far and we would just go straight to bed and forget it.

When Mark pulled into the garage, he practically ran over to my side of the car and pulled the door up and pulled me out like he was rescuing me. He immediately grabbed me and started to run his hands up the back of my dress.

He was voracious is his kissing. I could feel my heart rate increasing. A still voice told me to stop him. That voice has the *worst* timing. I ignored it, and Mark and I somehow made it up to the door that led to the house.

There was non-stop kissing all the way, from Mark fumbling with his keys to unlock the door, to us coming through the kitchen. He dropped the keys on the kitchen floor and didn't even bother to pick up them.

He was kissing my neck and he picked me up and put me on top of the kitchen island and he slid his hands on my knees and started pushing up my dress and I wrapped my legs around him.

He quickly moved his hands up and grazed my breasts. I got a chill up my spine. I debated whether or not to stop it. We both knew where it was going to lead. That's when we heard loud sirens. We stopped for a second and saw lights flashing through the windows.

I don't know how many more emergency vehicles passed by and I don't know where they were going. But it was enough to kill the moment. The pause gave me clarity, so I pushed him off and told him we'd better stop. I wanted to say 'go, go, go,' but I knew if I didn't stop it now, I wouldn't stop it at all.

I straightened my outfit and hopped off the counter. "If you don't leave me alone, I'm going to sleep with you."

"Geez, I wouldn't want that to happen," he said,

scratching his head.

"Mark, we'd better figure out where this is headed – quickly."

"I thought this was headed for the bedroom." He sounded out of breath.

"If you want this, you'll have to do something about this." I flashed him my empty left finger.

"Oh, good, I thought you were flipping me off."

I glared at him and he stopped trying to be cute. He exhaled, clenching his fists. His voice was sarcastic. "What do you want to do – get married?"

My shoulders drooped and I exhaled a sigh of disappointment. I turned and moved away toward my bedroom. "Goodnight, Mark."

He unclenched his fists and sighed. He lunged forward and pulled me back. "Do you want to marry me?" he asked seriously.

I looked at him. "I love you. And, *not* like I've loved other people. I mean, I'd give you a kidney. I'd push you out of the way of an oncoming car. I'd take a bullet...*love* you!"

He looked at me with his mouth open. That looked like it messed him up more than anything else that happened tonight. He looked like he was trying to process what I said.

"So, ask yourself, would you take a bullet for me, Mark? 'Cause I have people that would – for money. But would you take one for love? If not, then you shouldn't even be joking about getting married."

He smacked his hands on the counter and I went to bed.

I woke up the next morning and heard the coffee pot gurgling. I knew Mark was awake. He was reading the paper while standing at the island where he had held me the night before. "Good morning, Meg."

"Morning," I said with a smile, not knowing if this day would bring the end of us.

Mark's cell phone rang. "Excuse me. I don't know who would be calling me this early." It was his director. They were shutting down the set for a few days because of a tropical storm moving up the west coast towards Fort Myers. That meant we could stay in Miami for a few days if we wanted to – which would be safer than heading into a storm.

He came over to the table with my coffee and squatted down next to me. "I did a lot of thinking last night and I *would* take a bullet, Megan. And throw myself on a grenade, and step on a landmine, okay?"

"Really?" I asked in disbelief.

"Yeah. I mean, I'd rather use a stunt double. But, *yes*."

I threw my arms around him and kissed him.

"Since the shoot has been delayed for a few days, how about we go to South Carolina?"

I was leery. "South Carolina?"

"My brother and his wife are in town for the weekend and I want everyone to meet the girl I'd take a bullet for."

I leaned in and kissed him again. "So, I'm meeting the family?"

"I want them to meet you as soon as possible."

"Just one thing. I don't want you to tell them about the money, okay?"

"What's the big deal? *I'm* rich," he said.

"I would rather they not know, okay?"

"All right, but now we need to catch a flight."

"We can charter a jet from here. I don't want to be trapped in a car with you for ten hours!"

I called several charter companies and no one could get us up in the air until the next day. That's when I started telling them that the flight was for Mark Taylor. That worked! I was able to book a flight in the afternoon. Mark overheard this and loved the fact that my name meant nothing in this town, but his got the flight.

I called Carol to tell her I'd be away for a few days. She was happy. We wondered what his parents would be like. I was a little nervous. I knew this was a big deal.

When we arrived at the airport in South Carolina, the limo service was waiting. The drive to their house took about ten minutes through pretty scenery. Mark told me he had bought them a house, but this was not a house. It was a huge estate.

It was brick with huge white columns, like something out of *Gone with the Wind*. It had two massive staircases in the front that twisted out and then faced each other at the bottom. There were huge trees everywhere and there was a lot of shade. They must've had like twenty acres. It was really pretty.

The driver pulled up to the front of the house and stopped the car.

Mark warned me, "By the way, my mom doesn't know The Civil War ended."

I laughed. He didn't laugh. Great – I can only imagine how they're going to react when they find out they're harboring a Yankee!

The front doors opened and people started spilling out. The driver opened the trunk and handed our bags off to the butler. Mark's mother practically ran over him trying to greet us, while singing, "My baby boy, my baby boy…" over and over again.

She gave him a big hug, with a lot of rocking involved. He introduced me to his family. His brother, Adam, was there with his wife, Kim, and their kids Tiffany and Jeremy. Marion, his father, was the last to come out.

They all exchanged hugs, while the kids screamed, "Uncle Mark, Uncle Mark!" and then tackled him. "Did you bring us presents?"

"Yes!" he said, as he shook the kids off his arms. "Let Uncle Mark unpack his bags and then I will give you guys your presents, okay?"

"Yay!" they both cheered.

His mother, Georgia, came over and shook my hand with a limp handshake. She looked me up and down to size me up. She almost was able to pull off a smile, but not quite. She was very petite.

Her hair was too dark and looked like something from a movie from the 1940s. And she was so pale! She kind of reminded me of Joan Crawford. I could totally see her beating the *crap* out of someone with a wire hanger!

By contrast, his dad gave me a smile and wrapped my hand in both his big paws.

"This is my father, Marion," Mark said.

"Hey, it's John Wayne," I declared. You could see who Mark takes after.

His dad laughed. "Not many people your age know that was his real name."

Mark smiled at me and his mother just glared at Marion disapprovingly. His dad was tall and had strong features. He also had a little belly. I figured it was a good example of what Mark will look like when he's older. We all went inside.

Georgia showed me to my room and announced Mark

would be way down the hall. I just smiled. I opened up my overnight bag on the queen sized bed and started putting my clothes in the dresser.

Mark came and kissed me, and then Georgia walked in. She made a really big deal out of it, as if we were naked.

"Oh my, I am so sorry." She put the back of her hand over her forehead and turned away. Too bad there wasn't a fainting couch around – she would've collapsed on it.

"Mama, Megan's my girlfriend. We kiss."

"Yes, well, dinner will be ready in about ten minutes. So please wash up."

"Yes, mother." Mark said. She gave me a cold stare and clasped her hands behind her back as she walked out of the room. I think she may beat the crap out of *me* with a wire hanger!

"You call her 'mama,' huh? That's different."

Mark turned and smiled at me. "Yup. I'm so happy you're meeting my family."

"They seem thrilled," I said.

"C'mon, they are going to love you," he said.

"Where's the bathroom? And do I need a GPS to find the dining room?"

He laughed. "Look who's talking. Your house is bigger than this."

"I don't know, Mark. I feel pretty small in this house right now."

"Let's eat!" his mother called. Mark led me out to the dining room. I asked Georgia if she needed help. She was just as rude as could be when she said, "That's what servants are for."

"Okay," I said. Mark pulled my chair out for me and we all sat down.

Georgia asked, "So, Megan, what do your parents do?"

"They were killed in an accident seven years ago."

"Oh, I'm sorry. Mark didn't tell us. In fact," she snapped, "he didn't tell us much."

"What would you like to know?" The servants brought the first course and Georgia asked the kids to say grace. They did a sweet little prayer and then we all began eating our soup.

"What do you do for a living?" Georgia asked without looking up from her spoon.

"I own a diner at the beach."

There were polite nods all around the table, and then Georgia's disappointed response. "A diner, huh? That's nice." She turned to Mark. "So, Mark, how's the movie going?"

Mark tried to change the subject. "Did you know Megan and I first met seven years ago when she was working for Phillip Mason in Miami?"

She was interested again. "Oh! So you're an architect?"

"No. I did the marketing and public relations for the firm."

"And you run a diner now, instead?" she said, frowning at Mark.

Marion spoke up. "Megan, you said the diner's at the beach. Do you have an ocean view?"

"Yes, it's on the water."

"And you own the building? That's quite an accomplishment for someone your age to own commercial waterfront property."

"I guess," I said, feeling inadequate, which was funny. No one makes me feel like that now.

"Dad was a real estate broker before he retired," Mark

told me.

Adam spoke up. "So, it must be pretty exciting to date an international star like my brother, huh?"

"Yeah, it's nice." I said, shrugging, like it wasn't a big deal. They all looked at me like I was crazy. "I mean, I don't care that he's famous. I would love him if –"

"If he owned a diner?" Georgia asked.

"Mama! What's the matter with you?" Mark snapped at her.

"I hope if you have any intentions of marriage that you get a pre-nup." I started laughing. She glared at me. "You won't sign a pre-nup?"

"Yes, I would. Just to prove I don't care about money. What's his is his and what's mine is mine."

"Mama, that's ridiculous, she doesn't need to sign a pre-nup." Mark bit into his fried chicken.

"Oh, it's okay Mark. What they don't understand is, if I wanted to use you," I squeezed his leg, "it wouldn't be for your money." Mark gagged on his chicken.

"See that? She made him choke!" Georgia yelled.

"Are you okay, honey?" I asked. He swallowed his food and wiped his mouth with his napkin.

"I'm fine," he told everyone.

"Excuse me," Georgia said, "I'm getting one of my migraines," and she walked out of the room.

Marion turned to me. "Sorry, she gets a lot of those."

"I'm sure," I said.

Adam stated, "Well, I hope you're not after him for his money."

I laughed. "Didn't he pay for you to go to law school?" I asked. Mark laughed.

Adam looked down at his plate. "Yes, he did."

"Well, you don't need to worry about me," I said. "I

don't want his money." The rest of the dinner was quiet. I think Mark was irritated at the way everyone was treating me.

Everyone got up to look at old photo albums in the parlor and I asked if I could go in the kitchen to get a drink. I just needed a minute away from them. Marion came in the kitchen after me.

"Sorry about Georgia, Megan. Mark's her favorite."

"Look, I know I'm not like the other people he dates, but I love him and he loves me. It doesn't matter what anyone else thinks."

"You're right. I have to go to the store. Can I get you anything, Megan?"

"I hate to ask, but would you mind picking up some stevia for me? I need it for my coffee."

"Sure. I've seen it in the store. Can you tell them I ran out for a couple of minutes?" he asked.

I went back into the parlor where Mark was sitting with his brother and sister-in-law. Adam was telling a story about when they were teenagers.

He said he liked being the older brother because he could bet Mark five bucks to eat various things around the yard and Mark would always do it.

On one occasion it was a cricket. "Mark took that thing and chomp, chomp, chomp. And then he swallowed it. That's when I learned Mark would eat *anything* for five dollars."

"Can anyone break a twenty?" I asked straight-faced. Mark laughed really hard. "What? I owe your dad $10 for my stevia." Mark looked at me and shook his head. "He just went to the store," I said and pointed to the door. They all started laughing. I sat down, and we talked for a long time about Mark's childhood. Then they all took turns interrogating me.

Finally, Kim asked Mark to play something on the piano for us. We sat around him. Mark played "Maybe I'm Amazed" by Paul McCartney.

Georgia returned when she heard Mark at the piano. The whole time he was playing, he was looking at me and Georgia was looking at him. If looks could kill, I think Mark and I would both be dead. We sat and listened to Mark play a medley of songs.

Then Marion came back from the store and sat down with us. After listening for a few minutes, he turned to me. "So, Megan, are you from Florida?"

"No, I grew up in Massachusetts and then moved to Florida when my parents retired."

Georgia's eye twitched. "Massachusetts, huh?" She gave Mark a foul look.

"It's okay Mama. Megan's grandparents came to this country *after* The Civil War," Mark said, trying to reassure her.

"Really? That's nice." She stared at Mark. "So where did they come from?"

No way was I going to defer to Mark. I told her, "My dad's family is from Italy and my mom's side is from Ireland."

"So, you're Italian?"

"Yup. Half." Everyone was quiet. "The bottom half," I said, trying to break the silence. Mark laughed, but he was the only one. They didn't like Yankees, but I guess they *really* didn't like Italians.

Her nose in the air, Georgia said, "Well, we all went to Italy a few years ago and I have to say, the women were absolute whores. They kept trying to have sex with these men," she gestured to Mark, Adam and Marion, "for money. What do you think about that?"

"I say kudos to Italian women for getting paid for what they're good at." Everyone laughed now, except Georgia. Mark smiled at me. I think he was pleased I could handle myself. Georgia stood up and shook out her skirt. "My tea is ready." And she stormed into the other room.

"Wow," I said to Mark, "your mom and I are *totally* hitting it off. She's lovely."

"Sorry about that. She'll warm up to you."

"I don't think so." Mark's father went into the kitchen and came back a couple minutes later with Georgia. We heard some unintelligible mumbling, and she sat back down and gave me a look so cold, it would've killed a polar bear. So naturally, I smiled and waved at her.

Marion sighed. "Megan, can you help me with dessert?"

"Where are the servants?" I asked, raising an eyebrow questioningly at Georgia. Then I shook my head, "So hard to find good help." Mark laughed. I followed Marion into the kitchen.

"I'm glad you are assertive, Megan. You have to be tough to make it in this family. She's been tougher on you than most. She's afraid Mark's going to marry you and then we'll have a mixed marriage in the family."

I laughed a little. "You do know I'm white?"

"But you're not *Southern*." He handed me a tray of snacks and carried the tea tray into the sitting room. I followed him in a daze.

Mark sang another song, and then asked me to sit beside him on the piano bench and sing "You're The One." I told him I didn't want to sing in front of everyone but Mark's not very easy to say no to – trust me!

I reminded everyone Mark was the professional. But

we sang the song in perfect harmony. Sounded pretty good too, if I do say so myself. Everyone clapped, except Georgia.

I excused myself and went to the bathroom right off the kitchen. Mark followed me to the kitchen to get some water. Adam came too. He'd had drinks in his hand all night, getting louder and louder with every drink.

As I innocently put on my lipstick in the bathroom I could every word they were saying. At that point, I didn't know if I should stay in there or come out. I was involuntarily eavesdropping.

"Brother, you have your hands full with that one."

"I know she's feisty."

"I meant her breasts. Did you buy them? They're nice, man."

"What? You idiot! They're real." Mark drank his water.

"So, how is she?"

Knowing what he was implying, Mark said, "Fine. How are you?"

"I mean, in bed. How is it?"

I could hear the click of Mark's glass on the counter. "I haven't slept with her yet."

"Whoa! *People's* 'Sexiest Man Alive' can't close the deal, huh? How long have you two been together?" he asked Mark.

"Three months," Mark said.

"Hold on here, you've been together for three months and haven't gotten any of that yet? You know, they have pills for that now."

"Shut up. She's waiting until she's married."

He asked excitedly, "So, she's a virgin? Nice."

"No, she's not a virgin."

"So, she's having sex, just not with *you*?"

"No, keep your voice down. She's a born again Christian and can't have sex until she's married."

"Oh, geez. Now, I've heard it all. What are wasting your time for?"

"Adam, I love this girl. She makes me feel like a teenager again."

"I believe it. You weren't getting any *then* either," he said.

"You know, you're a real jerk."

"Thank you," Adam said with a laugh, as he hit Mark on the shoulder.

Kim came into the kitchen. "Hey Kim, Can you believe Mark and Megan haven't done it yet and they've been together for three months?" Adam added.

"Why not?" Kim asked.

"She doesn't want to have sex before she's married!" Adam said with a laugh.

"And you haven't dumped her yet? You must really love her."

Adam said, "Not as much as Mom." And they all laughed.

I came out of the bathroom and they look horrified. They had been talking about me the whole time and had no idea I was even there.

I got myself a glass of water and we all went back into the other room with everyone else. "So," Marion asked, "what are you going to do when Mark wraps up the movie?"

"We're just trying to enjoy every moment we have together now," I said. I would let Mark tell them we were planning on getting married.

"Megan is coming back to California with me," Mark

announced boldly.

Mark looked really annoyed at his family. They all looked at each other. I looked at my watch and yawned behind my hand. I wasn't tired, but I felt uncomfortable. I said goodnight and left. Mark caught up with me in the hall.

"Megan?"

"Good luck, Mark. That's a tough crowd." I said, looking back at the room they were in.

"Oh, they just need to get to know you," he said.

"Yeah, right. Goodnight, dear."

"Goodnight."

I closed my door and turned my iPod on. I didn't want to hear anything they were discussing.

 Half an hour later, there was a knock on my door.

"Who is it?"

"Mark."

I answered the door in my pajamas and took out my ear buds. "What's up?"

He kissed me and closed the door. He walked me to the bed and started kissing me aggressively. I put my hand on his chest. "Is there an asteroid coming?" I asked.

"I'm sorry. I just realized I don't care what anyone else thinks," he said.

"Oh, your family must've told you they don't like me."

"They just don't know you. Megan, I had no idea they were going to react like this."

"It's not your fault. I guess they just think they're protecting you."

"From the big, bad, half Italian," he said as he grabbed my hands.

"Don't forget 'whore.'"

"She didn't call you that!"

"Didn't she?" I asked.

"Not *directly*. Sorry, babe."

"So, what did they say exactly?"

"Mom thinks you just want me for my money."

I laughed.

"I know. Then she reminded me that my great granddaddy's daddy was killed by a 'Yankee' in the war."

I laughed again and rolled my eyes.

"Oh, then she said if we have kids, they'll be half-Yankee. Then I told her you couldn't even have kids, and then she accused me of trying to *kill* her with that information."

"Mark? Are you having second thoughts about me?"

"No, I'm having second thoughts about *them*!"

We laughed and cuddled very innocently on the bed. And then we both fell asleep – together, in my room.

When I woke up, it was already seven o'clock and sunlight was peeking through the curtains. I liked waking up with him, even though it appears he's a pillow-stealer.

"Good morning," he said.

"Good morning."

"Did you sleep okay?" he asked.

"Yeah, I don't even know what time we went to sleep."

"It was late," he said.

Of course, Adam was up early and knocking on the door. "Mark, did you finally get some? We know you're not in your room." Mark didn't answer, but he threw a shoe at the door. We heard Adam's laughter fading down the hallway.

"I guess I should get out of here before everyone

notices I'm not in my room," Mark muttered.

"Yeah. I'm just going to hop in the shower and get dressed."

He kissed me. "I'll see you after we shower." He wiggled his eyebrows at me. "You know, we could always conserve water and shower together?"

"We've already slept together, don't push it."

"But we didn't have sex. That proves we could shower together and nothing would happen." He grinned.

"Get out of here before I throw a shoe at *you*!" I said.

After I showered and got dressed, I put the finishing touches on my outfit – which included a Red Sox hat. We all met in the kitchen for breakfast. I was drinking my coffee at the counter, and Mark came up behind me and kissed my neck. "Good morning, baby."

"Good morning, Mark," I said, trying to act cool. Everyone else was already eating.

"Save it, we know you slept in the same room last night." Adam looked at me. "You're a very bad girl, Megan!"

"We were talking all night," I said in a sing-song tone.

Adam laughed. "Is that what you crazy kids call it nowadays?"

Kim said, "Oh, leave them alone, Adam."

"What are the plans for today?" Mark asked.

Marion said, "We thought the guys would play golf and the girls would go shopping," he said while staring at my hat.

Mark asked, "Is that all right with you, Megan?"

"Sure. You know I love to shop."

Georgia stopped dramatically, looked at my Red Sox hat and let out an audible, "Ugh."

Mark kissed me goodbye and we went our separate ways. Georgia, Kim and I went out to lunch and tried to converse. I struggled to find anything in common with them. Kim's family was from this area and her dad was some pillar of Charleston society.

And I was from a working class family, so naturally Georgia made sure I knew *they* were not from working class people. I did however learn all about 'The War of Northern Aggression.' For those of you who don't know, that's how many Southerners refer to The Civil War.

Then, the ladies took me to downtown Charleston and gave me a tour all of the buildings the 'Yankees' burned and/or bombed, and otherwise destroyed. They also told me stories of how the 'Yankees' raped and pilfered *all* of the residents.

It was quite educational. It could've been my imagination, but instead of making eye contact with me, it seemed they were staring at my Red Sox hat every time they said anything to me.

I was so glad none of them were alive when it actually happened because then they might have been *really* upset. I was starting to question if Mark was adopted.

We met the guys for dinner at some well-known seafood place downtown. Mark gave me quite a greeting. He leaned me back and planted one on me. It was sort of a spectacle, like a scene from one of his movies, but I didn't mind. "Did you have fun?" he asked.

I just smiled. What was I supposed to say? We all sat down and a waitress came to take our order.

"Hey, guess what?" Mark asked. "We saw a deer playing golf!"

"Really? How does a deer hold his clubs?" I asked. Everyone laughed, except Georgia. She just rolled her eyes and drank her tea. What a humorless woman!

"I mean, we saw a huge deer on the course while we were golfing. I think you knew what I meant." He smiled.

"What did you shoot, dear?" I inquired.

"An 87, but Dad was keeping score, so I think he added some of his strokes to my name."

"I confess; I used a Mulligan or two," Marion said.

"Yeah, Dad, like on every hole," Mark said. They all laughed.

The food came and we started eating. It was good. Mark looked at my plate. "Can I have a bite?" I gave him a forkful. "Oh, that is *so* good." Georgia glared at me. "Hey Mom, can Dad give you and Kim a ride back to the house? I want to take Megan somewhere."

"Sure. You can borrow the Jag, but be careful – I just had it detailed." She said as she gave me the evil eye!

Was this lady kidding? I owned a *Bugatti*! Get off your high horse – or Jag!

When we finished lunch, we started heading across town in Georgia's Jaguar. I kept asking where we were going, but he said he wanted to keep it a surprise. We pulled up to a gorgeous house on the ocean.

"We're here." He climbed out of the car and came around to open my door. Had he brought me to a friend's house? He put his arm around me as we walked up onto the porch.

"But where *is* here?"

"Well, since you and my mom are not exactly hitting it off, I thought maybe I'd buy this place so we could stay here. C'mon, let's take a look."

It was beautiful. It was three stories high with wrap-around porches. It was painted a lovely soft blue and it had a lot of character. It was fairly new construction but was built to look like one of the historic homes Charleston is famous for.

The front door opened and a woman stepped out onto the porch. "Mr. Taylor. Hi, I'm Christy." She shook his hand.

"Hi. This is my girlfriend, Megan."

"Hi, Megan. Nice to meet you. Let me show you around." Christy took us through every room. The main living area had an open-concept floor plan, with floor-to-ceiling windows looking out to the ocean.

The water was much darker here than at home – colder, in many ways. Then she took us upstairs into the master suite.

It was kind of hard to envision. There was no furniture in any of the rooms. Mark asked me what I thought.

"It's nice, Mark. But what are we doing here?"

He turned to Christy. "Can you excuse us for just a moment?"

"Sure. I have to make a phone call," she said, as she walked downstairs.

"This is for us," Mark said.

"I'm confused."

"I don't want you to be unhappy," he said.

"I'm not unhappy. I would be unhappy if you bought this house. How much is it?"

"They're asking five million."

"Why wouldn't you let me buy it then? Five million to me is a lot less than it is for you."

"This isn't a money issue, is it?"

"Not really." I went to the window, ran my fingers along the sill. "I appreciate you wanting to make me feel at home. But this doesn't feel like home to me."

"I want to buy this house for you. That way we wouldn't have to live with my parents when we stay in Charleston between my projects."

"Stay in Charleston?"

"Yeah. I mean, Charleston will always be home to me."

"That's funny, because I was thinking I'd be home for you, now."

He clenched his fists and exhaled, apparently trying to calm himself down. "I don't know what to do. This is where I always go in between projects. I've always imagined me bringing my wife back here to my family."

"Well, my family's gone. And being with a family that hates me seems worse than not having any family at all."

As we descended the stairs, he popped the palm of his hand pretty hard against the wall. He told the Realtor we were sorry, but we'd changed our minds.

The drive back to his parents' house was pretty quiet. I wondered if he was having second thoughts. Of course he was. How could he defy his family? How could he marry someone who came from above the Mason-Dixon Line?

It went against everything that was so ingrained in him. How could Mark be so different from his family? Would that mind frame come back to him with his return to Charleston? His accent was returning – why not the dislike of Northerners? I would constantly be on the defensive here.

After we returned to the house, we all talked for a little while and then I went to my room. Georgia seemed to be in a nicer mood. I think she could sense the tension between Mark and I. Mark kissed me goodnight, but he was kind of listless. I pulled out my iPad and decided to play a game to try and get my mind off this trip. I was concerned what was going to happen with me and Mark. This was not going according to the plan.

CHAPTER 9

Mark went in to his dad's study to talk to him. Apparently, Mark was voicing his concern over the future of our relationship, and whether or not his family would be able to accept me. A few minutes later, Mark came to my room and told me his father wanted to speak with us.

He was standing behind his desk, wiping his glasses on his shirt. He gestured for us to sit in front of his desk.

"Now, what's going on between you two?"

We both shrugged our shoulders.

Marion sat down. "Okay, Mark, what's the biggest problem with you and Megan?"

"Nothing! There's no problem."

"I sense some tension between the two of you."

"That would be sexual," I said.

Mark shot me a look, like he couldn't believe I said the word 'sexual' in front of his dad. "Megan!" Mark chirped.

"All right, what's going on with you two?"

"Megan won't have sex until she's married," Mark blurted out.

"Gee, that would have been a good thing when I was your age. Now, your generation wants to marry a seasoned pro. I just don't get you young people." Marion said shaking his head.

"Dad, it's been *three* months."

"Well, God forbid you have to wait until you get married, like we did!"

"And Megan hates it here. I tried to buy her a house and she said she didn't want it."

"I would've liked to have discussed it first," I said.

"Megan. I'm sorry for the way everyone is treating you. No one should be made to feel like an outsider here, just because of where they were born," Marion declared.

"You know how Mama is."

"Believe me, I know. A day doesn't go by that she doesn't remind me I was born in Connecticut."

"What?" I screamed with laughter. I put my left hand up to my head in disbelief.

"Your mom is just concerned Megan is after your money. No offense, Megan."

"Off the record – I have *way* more money than Mark does."

Marion seemed genuinely surprised. "Is that so?"

"She does," Mark said as he reached for my hand.

"Are you two good then?" Marion asked with a smile. "Marriage is about compromise. That's why the Bible says you leave your parents and *cleave* to your spouse. You need to live for each other and if Megan doesn't want to live here – don't! In the grand scheme of things, it's not a big deal. I would like to pray for the two of you." He laid his hands on us and said a nice prayer and asked God to bless our relationship.

Unbeknownst to us, Georgia was standing in the

doorway of the office, glaring at us. Needless to say, she was not happy Marion was praying for us. She looked at all of us and then continued walking down the hall.

I thanked Marion and he asked Mark to stay behind for a second so he could give him something. I waited down the hall, out of earshot.

★ ★ ★ ★ ★

Mark and I said goodnight to each other and went into our rooms. A little while later, I went to his bedroom. I listened at the door for a moment. I didn't want to wake him if he was sleeping.

When I didn't hear anything, I just tapped with my fingers. "It's me," I called softly, and the door opened.

He said, "I was praying."

That was a surprise. "You were? What were you praying about?"

"I was asking God to give me a sign."

"And then I knocked on the door?"

"Yeah, it's okay you interrupted though. I wanted to talk to you. Sit down." I squinted my eyes, wondering if I *was* the sign. We sat on the bed and he held my hand. "Look, Megan, I know I don't want to break up with you."

"I didn't know you were contemplating that."

"This isn't how I pictured this weekend going. I never imagined my family wouldn't accept you."

"Have you met them before this weekend?"

He laughed.

"Mark, some things are worth waiting for."

"I know. I...just...I'm not good at waiting."

"You're not the only one suffering here. Look at you.

You're everything I've ever wanted and I can't do what feels natural to me. Believe me, this is not easy for me either," I said.

"Where do we go from here?" he asked.

"I don't know, Mark. I don't know if there'll be a happy Hollywood ending for us," I said. He put his head in his hands. "What I do know is we don't have to decide this tonight."

He kissed me. "I'm not ready to give up."

"Good." And I stood up and went to bed.

The next morning, we went to church. There were a lot of people there who knew Mark from childhood. Everyone was nice.

They kept asking him if I was his wife. He would smile and say "not yet." Georgia didn't like that, but I thought it was funny.

After the service, the pastor came up to us. He shook Mark's hand. "Well, how's my favorite movie star?"

"Good, Pastor Dan. This is Megan."

I shook his hand. "Nice to meet you."

"Mark, this is your wife."

"Oh, she's my girlfriend."

"I'm not asking you. I'm telling you. This is the woman you're going to *marry*."

My jaw dropped. "What?" Mark asked.

"You two belong together. Please excuse me; *my* wife is waiting for me. I promised her lunch at The Outback. She gets cranky if she doesn't eat." He turned to me, "It was nice meeting you, Megan. Goodbye, everyone."

Mark and I stared at each other. Georgia started walking towards the car. Wordless, we followed her out to the car. Mark and I got in the back of Georgia's Jag and smiled at each other in disbelief. Mark grabbed my hand and kept looking at me. Marion and Georgia got in the car and drove us back to their house.

We ate lunch outside. It was a warm day with little humidity. Everyone sat at the table, while the kids ran around the yard with the planes Mark brought for them. After we finished eating, Mark and I packed our bags and said goodbye to everyone.

"Don't lose that box, Mark."

"What box?" I asked him.

He shook his head. "It's nothing."

The limo came and picked us up and we waved goodbye as we drove away. When I looked out the back window everyone was gone, except Georgia. She just stood there and watched us drive off.

While we rode back to the airport, we started to talk.

"That was a weird trip," Mark said.

"Which part?" I asked.

"I think you know what I'm talking about," he said as he turned towards me.

"Does it make you nervous?" I asked.

"No, I'm actually okay."

"Well, how long are we going to put off the inevitable?" I asked.

"What do you mean?"

I looked at my watch. "If we leave for Vegas now, we can be naked by dinner."

He leaned closer and turned my face toward his. "Are you serious?"

"I don't know. Does that sound like a *good* plan?"

He thought about it for a minute. "No, that's crazy, right?"

"Yeah, that would be pretty crazy." But I looked him up and down, and blew my breath out. I didn't know how much longer I could hold out.

"I'm not opposed to eloping, it's just – I mean, Vegas. It is kind of ridiculous. I mean, why don't we just get married in Florida, on the beach?"

"I think the beach would be perfect," I said.

"Okay, the beach it is," he said.

"We'd have to get a marriage license and there's a three-day waiting period in Florida."

"That's all right. I think we can wait three more days." He smiled nervously at me. We got to the airport and the flight attendant threw our bags into the plane.

We sat down and strapped ourselves in. I took Mark's hand as we started to taxi. Everything was going to be all right! He lay back in his seat and closed his eyes. Look at this man! He is beautiful. He is perfect for me in so many ways. I never believed I could love anyone like this.

The flight back was quiet. His hand had gone slack in mine as he fell asleep. I didn't mind – it gave me time to think.

Were we serious about getting married? I didn't know how serious he was. Heck, I didn't even know how serious I was. Did I really want to marry someone famous?

That would mean a lifestyle in the media that I couldn't avoid, even on a small scale. Granted, he would be the focus, but still. Could I trust him not to leave me, especially given the revolving relationships in the entertainment industry?

How would I feel about somebody kissing Mark and pretending to have sex with him all day? That was weird. I'm not a jealous person, but I sure didn't like the idea of it.

And, his family – yikes! They hate me! Would they

learn to like me? Probably, when they find out how much money I'm worth. Then, they'll finally accept me. Hypocrites! Imagine, Marion being from Connecticut!

Mark had to be up really early the next day, so we flew to the executive airport in Fort Myers on US-41. The limo dropped him off at his rental house. He kissed me goodnight and said he would call the next morning when they were finished on the set.

I figured he would call the next day and say he'd changed his mind. But when he called, he said he wanted to go the courthouse and apply for a marriage license. I was shocked. He was actually serious about it! *People*'s 'Sexiest Man Alive' really wanted to marry me.

I picked him up and we drove downtown. "Are you sure about this?" I asked.

"Yes. Why, are you not sure?" he asked, nervously.

"I'm sure it's what I want, but I have to reiterate, I don't believe in divorce," I said firmly.

"Great, neither do I. That's why I never married anyone before." We went to the courthouse and applied for the license, after we paid everyone in the office not to leak it to the media.

The Clerk of Court asked if she could get a picture with us and then she wished us good luck. We ate lunch and then went back to my house.

A few days after we returned, our lives became normal again. And our summer romance entered the month of October. Mark's movie was literally a week from wrapping up.

We still hadn't committed to a date for the ceremony. I

was worried about what was going to happen in the future. We didn't even know where Mark was going to wind up.

If he got the television series, at least we would have a reasonably normal life and we'd still be living in Florida. We did, at least, manage to resolve the Charleston issue. Mark said he was getting nervous about our impending nuptials and he overreacted. He said if I preferred to live in Florida in between his projects, he was fine with it – all that mattered was that we stayed together.

Mark was needed on the set and I had to get ready for the gala my parents had held every year. They had volunteered for many years at the Guardian Ad Litem program, which helps abused and neglected children get an independent advocate to look out for their needs.

My parents loved children and threw these annual fundraisers at one of the hotels on the beach. It was a tradition I continued, to honor their memory.

People don't realize there's a direct correlation between the economy and child abuse. The recession had really strained the economy in Fort Myers. We had one of the worst housing and job markets in the nation. I had to do something that mattered.

It was sometimes hard for me to remember there were people out there with real problems. Giving back to these children reminded me of all the stories I'd heard from my parents.

Stories about kids that would never get a fair shot at life because they came from families that were beyond broken.

I showered and slipped into my dress, wishing Mark could go with me. But they were re-shooting some scenes on the beach that the director didn't like, and he had to be there. I did my hair and make-up – except for my lipstick. I slipped on my jewelry. Mark was watching television in the living room, but he stood up when I came out.

"Wow," he said. "You look –"

"Alluring? Fetching? Ravishing?"

He chuckled. "Conceited," he added to the list, smiling.

"That too." I smiled.

He came over to me. "I have to tell you, I really don't like your necklace."

I touched it. "What's the matter with it?"

He walked over to his duffle bag and pulled out a black velvet box. "I think this would look better."

I opened the box. It was a huge bib necklace of diamonds and sapphires. He took the other necklace off and placed it in the box, and draped the new one around my neck. I walked over to a mirror and touched the necklace. He was right behind me.

"You really shouldn't have done this," I said, turning to look at him.

"Since I couldn't be there, I didn't want you to forget about me."

"Thank you, Mark. It's really beautiful." He kissed my neck. "Now, I have to change my earrings. I'll be right back." I walked into the bedroom and found my sapphires.

"Are you going to miss me?" he asked as I came back out, putting my earrings on.

"Are you kidding me? I don't want to go anywhere without you, especially when I look this cute." I went to him and rested my forehead against his chest. I sighed.

"What's the matter?"

I looked up at him. "I'm spending a hundred grand on

this event. Rich people love their parties, and then you bought me this expensive necklace. I feel like a hypocrite. I mean, I could have just written them a check instead."

"Listen, you're going to bring in thousands of dollars for those kids. What's really bothering you? Are you upset I can't be there?"

I turned away, fidgeting with my bracelet. "Carol told me Phillip bought a ticket; he's going to be there tonight. I don't know what he's up to."

"I'm sorry I can't be there, babe." He put his arms around me.

"I know. I just wanted you to know." I pulled away and kissed his cheek. "I'll be okay. Carol will be there."

"He's married now, anyway," Mark said.

"Actually, they're divorced."

"Ooh. So he's coming back to try and win your heart?"

"I don't know. I gave him money years ago when his business was failing."

"How much money did you give him?" he asked. I raised my eyebrows. "You're right, sorry. It's none of my business. Forget I asked."

He looked at his watch. "Shoot, I really have to get going," he said.

"I feel so much more for you than I ever did for him," I said, walking him to the door. "A small part of me died every time I lost someone in my life. But you've made me alive again."

He kissed me, soft and slow. "I'm sorry, Megan, I really do have to go. I love you." He pushed the door open. "I will call you as soon as we're done. What time do you think you'll be home?"

"I have no idea. Maybe midnight?"

"I'll call you later." He ran down the steps.

I put my lipstick on as my limo pulled into the driveway. It took only about ten minutes to get there. I thought about what I would say when Phillip approached me. I didn't want to be alone with him for even one minute. His brother still lived in Fort Myers.

It was rumored Phillip never recovered financially from Julian's dirty dealing and he was looking to marry money to maintain his lifestyle.

And then I remembered Joseph Carr also bought a ticket to the gala. No doubt he would write another horrible story about me. The last thing Mark and I needed was a story about us. Maybe it was just as well he couldn't come.

The night started out as usual with people casually drifting in and out of the doors. The band I had hired was the same one that had been playing at this function for the last few years.

They were excellent and they played exactly what I wanted them to.

Carol exclaimed about the decorations. There were fine linens, white roses, balloons and glitter everywhere. Carol told me I looked like Cinderella. I guess that's why the place looked like my fairy godmother threw up on it. It was kind of over-the-top.

Well into the evening, I stood at the center of a large crowd. Several people had asked me to tell the story of the attempted carjacking.

"Then I said to him, 'depress the clutch all the way to the floor with your left foot and with your right hand,' – I pulled out my gun and pointed it at him, I said – 'pick up my phone and call 911.'" Everyone laughed. I finished the story and the people just ate it up. It is a great story – if it didn't happen to *you*!

The crowd started to disperse. I took a sip of my drink and said to Carol, "I'm so sick of telling that story."

Carol smiled while looking at the crowd. "I know."

"Can I go home now?" I couldn't wait to get out of there.

Carol said no.

"C'mon, Carol, you can handle the fundraising without me."

"No, Megan. They come to hear your stories, not mine."

"Well, can't say I blame them there!" I laughed.

Carol said, "Be nice or I'll auction you off for a date."

"Funny," I said. I was looking at Carol when Phillip came over to us. He'd shaved his beard. He looked a lot younger. He looked really good. Then again, every man looks good in a tuxedo. He took my hand and kissed it.

"Hi, Megan."

"Phillip." I nodded coldly.

"Hi, Carol. How are you?" he asked.

"Great, Phillip. How's the architecture *biz*?" she asked politely, but she really didn't care. She never liked Phillip!

"Good, it's good." He turned back to me. "God, you look great, Megan."

Carol excused herself. "I'm going to the powder room."

I frowned at her for leaving me.

"Would you please dance with me?" he asked. "It's a slow dance."

"Sure." He set my glass down on a nearby table and we started to dance.

"You are still the most beautiful woman in a crowd."

"And the richest," I said, as I looked around for someone more interesting to talk to.

"You know I never cared about money."

"Oh yes, Phillip, I know." He always loved money and we both knew it. "What are you doing here, Phillip?" I asked.

"I made a mistake."

"Which one?"

"Everything. I shouldn't have broken things off so abruptly. I loved you and I treated you badly."

"That was seven years ago. I'm over it," I said, bored.

"I should've never let you go."

"What do you want, Phillip?"

"I have kids now, Megan. It doesn't matter anymore that you can't have them. Let's be honest, you're not getting any younger. You still want to get married, don't you?"

"Ugh. Is this the way you apologize, really?"

"I still care about you."

"I can tell," I said.

"Plus, my brother told me you're a Christian now and you can't have sex until you're married. That's crazy, Megan. Who's going to marry you without having sex with you? We've already done it, so I'm comfortable marrying you."

"Well, far be it from me to make you leave your comfort zone." I started walking away.

"I'm just saying, I'm offering to marry you as you are." He winked at me. "You remember how good we were together?"

"Not really," I said, trying to remember anything good about our relationship.

I wondered which of us should be more embarrassed; Phillip for his obvious desire to marry money or me for spending any part of my life with this guy. I couldn't remember one good thing about him.

What did I ever see in this guy? Perhaps I was once as superficial and preoccupied with money as he was.

Had I really been willing to tolerate someone who didn't love me just to get what I wanted? Is that who I used to be?

The crowd started to get loud and I didn't know why. Then the people nearest the entrance started cheering. I saw Carol talking to a man in an old-fashioned Air Force uniform and gesturing toward me.

My heart lifted when I realized it was Mark. I could feel my heart pounding.

Phillip took my chin and turned my face until our eyes met. Then he whispered to me, "Do I need to remind you how hot it used to be between us?"

I jerked away. "Sorry, Phillip. I don't have three minutes right now."

"Megan, c'mon, I screwed up. But we're older now. It could work."

"Gee, Phillip, I thought tonight was just a charity for kids; lucky me!" I could see Mark making his way slowly through the crowd, as the band started playing a cheesy love song.

I rolled my eyes when they announced Phillip had dedicated to me. Phillip took my arm, pleading with me to give him another chance.

Mark was coming towards us and saw Phillip grab my arm. He started running towards me to intervene, but then he saw my security team swoop in. I threw Phillip's hand off me and my security team surrounded me.

"Do we need to remove this gentleman, Ms. Pagano?" the guard asked me.

"No, he's fine, thank you." No reason to make more of a spectacle than necessary. I turned back to Phillip. "Don't ever touch me again," I hissed.

The security guard said to Phillip, "Keep your hands to yourself or next time I won't be so gentle."

Mark came up then, eyes narrowed on Phillip. "Are you okay, Megan?" He put his arm around me.

"What is Mark Taylor doing here?" Poor Phillip, he didn't stand a chance. "You two are together?" He burst into laughter. "That's priceless. Megan, you can't be serious about him? He could never love you like I would!"

"I'm counting on that," I said sweetly.

"Are you having sex with him? 'Cause there's no way he'd be interested otherwise," Phillip said.

Mark left my side and got in his face. "You're not behaving like a gentleman, Phillip. You can either leave or I can teach you a lesson on how to behave in front of a lady."

"A lady. Are you talking about Megan!?" Phillip laughed.

By now, there was a crowd forming. It was getting loud, and people were starting to point and move in closer.

"Megan, look at this guy. He's an alcoholic! He *threw up* on you!" Phillip raged.

"At least I didn't leave her because she can't have *kids*!" Mark said.

"You told him about that?" Phillip's face was red, but

I didn't know if it was from anger or embarrassment.

"I could've told him *worse* things, Phillip."

"Phillip, you're making a spectacle of yourself," Mark snapped.

A woman yelled, "Hit him, Mark." The crowd was getting louder and louder. I felt like I was in West Side Story, minus the weapons and music of course.

Mark clenched his right hand into a fist. Security looked at me questioningly and I shook my head no. I knew this was something Mark needed to take care of.

Phillip took a quick look around. We were surrounded by the enthusiastic crowd. There was nowhere for him to run. "You know what, Mark? You can have her. I already got what I wanted from her. And I didn't have to *marry* her!"

My eyes widened and before I knew it, Mark clocked him. And I mean good, too. His nose was bleeding.

"You broke my nose," he yelled.

"Cheer up, it doesn't look much different," Mark snipped. The crowd started clapping. I nodded for security to take Phillip out.

"Well, that'll be on the front page," Mark said.

"Yup," I said.

"Screw it," he said. Then he grinned, and he leaned me back and kissed me. Then he called to the crowd, "Who wants to hear some music?" The crowd burst into applause.

Mark hopped on stage and talked briefly with the bandleader. Then Mark grabbed the microphone.

"I know many of you call her 'The Lottery Heiress,' but I call her the love of my life. Megan, please come up here." Everyone clapped and hollered. Reluctantly, I went up on stage. He took my hand and started singing to me.

He was twirling me around and didn't take his eyes off me once. I was totally embarrassed. The cat was out of the bag now. Everyone in the room knew we were in love. The local media would have a field day. But Mark didn't seem to care. He sang another song and then we walked over to the bar to get a drink.

I asked for two ginger ales in champagne glasses, and I handed one to him.

"You know I don't drink."

"It's just ginger ale. If you don't look like you're drinking, people are going to be handing you alcohol all night."

"Ma'am, I'm flying out to tomorrow and I don't know if I'll make it back." He grinned at me.

"You know, my nana told me that line worked on a lot of women." For a moment, I wished it was the '40s and he was flying out – what a night that would be! "You *are* pretty irresistible in that uniform, Lieutenant."

"I wish I could say the same. That dress is so ugly, I just want to take you home and rip it off you."

"Well, sorry to disappoint you, my heart belongs to an actor."

"Ooh, that's riskier than being in love with an airman," he said.

"Probably! Mark, obviously, I'm happy to see you, but how are you here?"

"Vanessa was drunk again and passed out when she finally showed up on the set."

"Oh, good. I mean, not for her liver, but for me. I'm sorry that little escapade is probably going to go viral."

"It's all right."

We walked over to the hors d'oeuvres table. A few

people came up to Mark and said they really liked his performance.

We picked up some wine crackers and caviar and stood talking to some of the guests. Then I saw Joseph Carr some way off, conversing with one of our big donors. Imagine being able to tell the world Mark Taylor had fallen in love with someone he can't have sex with. It would be fodder for all the late night talk shows and Joseph's name would go national.

I managed to avoid him the rest of the night, until we were about to leave. He came up to Mark and me, shaking his iPad. "You all make me want to vomit with your candy-covered publicity stunts. Who would actually believe Mark Taylor would fall for someone he can't even screw? I'm not buying it."

"Watch your mouth," Mark threatened him.

"What are you going do, hit me too? Go ahead, and then I'll have a follow-up story from the hospital."

He looked at me, "Who is this jerk?"

"Joseph Carr," I said quietly.

"You know what? You're a real jerk," Mark said coldly. Joseph just laughed.

It was time. I had a confession for Joseph that would rock his world. And, I hoped, put an end to his harassment.

"How's your daughter?" I asked.

"Excuse me? I don't see how that's any business of yours."

I showed him my arm, which had minor scars from the procedure that had saved his daughter's life.

"These make it my business."

"No, I don't believe you! You'll say anything to stop me from running this story."

"Do you want to take my picture and show it to Liz?" I asked.

"I don't believe it," he said again. He was turning into 'The Incredible Hulk' with his rage – well, minus the green skin and big muscles. But he definitely had the anger part.

"Why would you do that?" he whispered, gritting his teeth.

"I didn't want you to go through the pain of losing someone you love. You're not as strong as I am."

"Why? After all I've written about you." A tear started rolling down his face. He wiped it away with the back of his hand.

I shrugged. Mark stared at me in disbelief. I had never told anyone what I had done, not even Carol. "Matthew 5:44, love your enemies."

Joseph hugged me. "I am so sorry."

"I forgive you. But now I am asking you…please, bury the story."

"Fine, I won't run the story. But there are hundreds of people here. It's probably already on social media." He turned to go.

"Thank you, Mr. Carr," I said.

Mark looked at me, "I can't believe you saved his daughter's life."

"I just realized something," I said, faking surprise.

"What?" he asked.

"I'm *amazing*," I said.

He laughed. "And humble, too."

We headed down the steps to the limo. "How did you get here, anyway?" I asked.

"I walked. We were shooting right there." He pointed to the beach in front of the building.

"Well, this is my ride," I said.

"Then let's go back to your place." As soon as we were seated in the car, he kissed me, and then took my hand. "Man, it usually takes a lot to get me angry, but I wanted to kill Phillip tonight."

He looked down, rubbing my hand. "I just got a call from my agent. I have to go back to L.A. for a few days for a press junket, then to New York to do some late night shows and then I'm off to Italy."

"I don't want you to leave," I said clinging on to his arm.

"Come with me. I've got a huge house in L.A., there's plenty of room for you."

I touched his face. "I have to be married, Mark."

"We'll get married as soon as I get back from Italy. It will be a lot easier. Honestly, every minute of my life is booked until then."

"I can't go back to L.A. with you, Mark. I think I should wait until you come back from Italy."

He looked up toward the sunroof. "Are you sure He can see everything?"

"Yup, I'm pretty sure."

He kissed me again. "Then He can see how much I love you, Megan."

When we got back to the house, he sat down on the couch and promptly fell asleep. He'd been up for almost 24 hours because of Vanessa causing delays. I laid a blanket over him and went to sleep in my room.

When we woke up in the morning, we decided to go for a swim in the pool while the coffee was brewing. We swam about 30 laps, then put on robes and drank our coffee.

"You know, sometimes I'm on the set and I find my

mind wandering. What is Megan doing right now? Is she thinking about me?"

"I am. Always."

He took me in his arms and kissed me. He looked at his watch and went in the other room to change clothes. He drank his last sip of coffee.

"Oh, I have to go. I'll call you soon as we're done today."

"No breakfast?"

"No, they have food on the set."

He kissed me. "I love you."

"I love you, too." I grabbed his arm and kissed him one more time.

"Don't do that again or I won't leave." I did it again and then he walked out the door. He came back right away and smiled. "I need a ride. Do you want to come back to my trailer with me?"

I laughed. "Man, if I had a dollar for every time a guy asked me back to his trailer!" He laughed. "Actually, if you want to take a car, I promised Carol I'd open for her today."

"Oh, okay." We walked down to the garage. He took the keys to my Mustang. I had mace on a key chain that also had a keychain that read, "WWJD?" He found this amusing.

"You have mace on a 'What Would Jesus Do' keychain?"

"Well, Jesus wouldn't mace people, but I would."

He kissed me goodbye and then left. I spent the day at my laptop.

I wanted to write a story about coping with loss, but instead I wound up writing about how I fell in love with a Hollywood bad boy who didn't seem so bad after all. The only problem was I still wasn't sure how it was going to end.

CHAPTER 10

Another tropical storm was churning across from the east coast. It was raining – hard. I was leafing through a design magazine and listening to my iPhone on the stereo, waiting for Mark. He'd called earlier to say his shoot would be late. When the doorbell rang, I ran to open it. It was 10:00.

It's funny. If you know me, you know I don't remember high levels of detail. But I remember everything about that night. I remember the way he smelled and how he kissed me, and even the song that was playing. It was "The Rain Song" by Led Zeppelin.

He was soaked. He didn't even say hi. As soon as I opened the door he was all over me. I remember it like it was yesterday. He kissed me, hard and deep. We kind of crab-walked over to the couch and he kissed every inch of my face, my ears, my neck. We didn't say anything to each other. We didn't need to talk.

He was so wet from the rain, I got soaked from just being pressed up against him. He kicked off his shoes. He ran his hands up my back and down my sides. "Tell me when to stop," he said. I didn't want him to, so I said nothing, even though I knew it was escalating – quickly. He looked at me hard and said, "I swear I'm going to die if I don't make love to you right now."

I tried to say no, but what came out was, "Well, I don't want you to *die*!"

I took off his long sleeved shirt, though he still had his t-shirt on. He kissed my neck. I got a chill. I kept thinking I'd just let it go on for another minute and then I'd stop him. But that minute turned into a very long time. He pulled back and looked at me for a sign. Still I didn't stop him. He stopped kissing me, stood up and grabbed the car keys out of his pocket and threw them on the side table. He then pulled me off the couch towards him. "Let's go upstairs," he said.

We practically ran up the stairs. I remember how cold the marble was on my feet. When we got to the top step, he led me quickly into the bedroom. He sat down on the bed and pulled me on top of him. He ran his hand from my neck to the middle of my chest to my stomach. That little angel popped up on my right shoulder, and you know I knocked it right off.

His hair was getting really messed up from me running my hands through it. His breath was getting heavy and I could feel things progressing to a point of no return. The lightning was reminding me of my wicked intentions every time it flashed. The thunder was reprimanding me with every boom. "Tell me when to stop, Megan," Mark whispered again.

I didn't say anything. I just let him keep kissing me. He slid his hands from my knees to my thighs. Still I did not say a word. I took off his t-shirt and he took off my sweater. I had never kissed him like that, in my room, skin on skin. I tried to muster up the strength to push him off or make him leave, but I didn't want him to.

His lips pressed against mine, urgently. I lay down on the bed and he climbed on top of me. His mariner link gold necklace was touching my neck. I ran my hands up and down his back, his sides, and his butt. He kissed my stomach and worked his way up. "Tell me when to stop."

I knew I wasn't going to tell him to stop, because I would've done it by now. I already decided – I wanted him and I was going to have him, even if it was wrong.

Mark kissed me and then lifted his head up and looked at me. "I'm not going to ask you to tell me when to stop anymore."

I said, "I'm not going to tell you to stop anymore." He raised his eyebrows. I just pulled him to me and aggressively kissed him. Well, that was it. We both knew it was going to happen. I'd think about the repercussions tomorrow. All of a sudden, lightning flashed in the room, followed by a scary 'boom.'

My fingers were on the button of his jeans when he suddenly flinched, pulling away from me. He glanced around the room. This time, a flash of lightning filled the room and the loudest 'boom' I'd ever heard.

"What's the matter?" I asked.

He said, "Nothing," but he seemed distracted. He started to kiss me again and then came a blinding flash of lightning, followed by the most terrifying 'boom' I had ever heard in my life. He jumped and actually fell off the bed. He let out a whimper and scrambled to his feet.

"This was a bad idea, Megan." He started gathering his clothes up aggressively. I sat up, watching in disbelief. He grabbed his shirt and headed down the stairs for the living room.

I ran after him. "Mark, what's wrong with you?" He

put his t-shirt on and he jammed his feet into his loafers like there was a fire or something. Then he headed out the door.

"Mark?" I literally chased after him.

"Don't – don't say anything. I need some time to figure this out, okay?"

"Figure what out? I love you. I *want* you."

"I know. I just – we can't have sex, okay? I'm sorry; this isn't going to happen between us."

I started crying, but I somehow stayed calm. I'd known this day was coming, just not like this.

"Goodbye Mark." When he looked at me, his eyes were wild. He lowered his head, and then looked up at me again. I thought he was going to say something to change things, but he just walked out and walked home in the pouring rain.

At Big Mama's the next day, Carol asked, "Did you and Mark do anything last night?"

"Yeah. Actually we broke up." Everyone came over and said they were sorry, except for Bud.

"A guy like that is used to getting what he wants. You know, we used to have a name for girls like you who didn't have sex before marriage."

I rolled my eyes and folded my arms. "What?" I asked, totally annoyed by his comments.

"Nice girls."

"Oh yeah? What did you call the girls who did?" I asked.

He said, reminiscing, "Fun!"

"Well gee, thanks for that pearl of wisdom, Bud."

Carol put her arm around me and started walking me back to my office.

Bud yelled after us, "I never liked that guy, Megan."

Carol turned around and shook her head at Bud. She shut the door behind us. I sat in my chair. I asked Carol how she was, and she told me her brother-in-law was in hospice and was about to die. Then I felt guilty that I hadn't even prayed for the guy or his family. I had let Mark dominate every part of my life.

"What happened with Mark?" Carol asked. "Was it because you wouldn't sleep with him?"

"No, I, uh, tried to have sex with him and he left."

She got angry. "What? Megan, you're not supposed to do that and you know it. What happened?"

"He told me we couldn't have sex and then he said it was over."

"Hold up. He left *after* you made it clear you were willing?" she asked.

I nodded. "Yeah. He left right after that."

"Are you sure he knew you wanted to have sex?"

"Trust me, he knew, Carol." I put my elbows on the desk and buried my face in my hands. "Maybe he wasn't in love with me, because he got out of there pretty fast."

"Megan, I saw the way that boy looked at you. He loves you all right. Maybe he didn't do it *because* he loves you!"

"I'm not so sure about that anymore." I looked at her and shook my head. "I should've known this was going to end badly."

"Just let it cool down and then see what happens. He can't just walk away and forget about you. He wanted to *marry* you. He's just scared honey," she said.

"I wish I could believe that. But you didn't see him. He was like a different person. It was like I disappointed him. I've turned into something I hate – a hypocrite."

"Megan, he wants to do the right thing. He sees people

compromising their values all the time. You were the one person who made him wait and he fell in love with you because of it. He got to know someone, for real." She wrote something on my notepad. "I think you need to look this up." She gave me a sympathetic smile.

"What is this?" I asked as I picked up the note. It read, *I Corinthians 10:13.*

"It'll work itself out, Megan."

"I don't think so, Carol. I think I really blew it." She put her hand on my shoulder for a moment, and then walked out.

After she left the office, I reached for the Bible I keep on my desk and I looked up the passage. I sat there just meditating for a very long time. There was no sense in me going home to a huge house just to be alone.

A few hours later, one of our regular customers came in and said Joseph Carr had a big blow-up with his editor at the paper over Mark and me breaking up. Apparently, the editor wanted Joseph to write a story about it and he refused. Joseph called me 'old news.' I called the paper to confirm Joseph quit over it and he had.

News of this came to the diner pretty quickly. When I was speaking with Carol, I found out the paper had just been bought out by one of the volunteers from Guardians Ad Litem, who had attended my parents' gala a couple of days earlier. Her name was Candy and she was from a huge media mogul family. And she really liked me.

I called her and strongly recommended a personnel change for the paper, and she agreed. Joseph Carr was announced as the new editor, and he promised to run a paper with honesty and integrity and no bias – the way journalism used to be. Apparently, someone told Joseph I was responsible for the change. He tried to call me but I wasn't talking to anyone. I couldn't. I was so depressed, I hardly left the house.

Carol came by the house and tried to cheer me up. I was a total mess. I was crying. "What's the matter?" she asked.

"Can't I get emotional watching television? I have very deep emotions." I blew my nose.

Carol looked at the television. "Honey, that's *NASCAR*."

I went into the kitchen and got a jar of Nutella out of the cabinet and a very large spoon.

Carol asked, "What are you doing?"

"I am making myself feel better."

"You're going to get fat again."

"I don't care. No one's ever going to see me naked again, anyway." I shoved the spoon into the jar, scooped out a huge spoonful and swallowed it.

"Megan, put the spoon down. You don't want to do this. You can't solve your problems by eating."

"No, I can't." I shoved another spoonful of Nutella into my mouth.

Carol put her hands on her hips and scolded, like she was my mother. "You're going to raise your blood sugar levels, you little diabetic."

"Ooh, tough talk from the leader of 'Heck's Angels.'"

"Megan, obviously you don't want company right now." She grabbed her purse and headed for the door.

"Carol, I love him," I said with a sob.

She came back and hugged me. "I know, honey." There were tears in her eyes, too.

A news alert came on. There was a new tropical storm threatening us. There were so many tropical storms this year, they were on the letter 'M.' Awesome – this storm was being called, "Tropical Storm *Mark*." How appropriate. Carol and I just looked at each other.

★ ★ ★ ★ ★

A few nights later, I happened to catch Mark on a late night talk show. He was talking about his movie that was coming out, *Prying Eyes,* in which he starred with his ex-girlfriend, Sophia Rae. When Mark was asked if they were back together, Mark said he was not involved with anyone at the moment. He talked about being voted 'Sexiest Man Alive' and being single.

The women in the audience were screaming and it made me feel sick to my stomach. It was like watching a complete stranger. It seemed like the past three months never existed at all. He had on clothes I'd never seen and he had a different haircut.

The ticker on the bottom of the television said "Tropical Storm Mark" was officially "Hurricane Mark" now, but it looked like it was turning west and would only be dropping rain bands on our coast. At least there was good news about something.

I clicked the channels and a tabloid show was saying Mark was back with Sophia. They even had pictures of them together. I shut the television off. I curled up on the couch hugging a big pillow and I prayed. I asked God to forgive me for what I did.

I'd never understand how I had misjudged things by thinking Mark was the one. Maybe I just wanted him to be the one. I fell asleep crying and continued crying for the next few days. My eyes looked so puffy, I didn't even leave my house.

I woke up to heavy wind and rain. They were causing

the palm fronds to smack across my windows. I looked out the window and there was debris all over my usually perfectly manicured lawn. The rain was so loud on the roof, it sounded like it was literally raining cats and dogs. All of a sudden, someone came banging on the front door. What could possibly be so important? It was Carol. "Megan, I have been trying to call you for hours."

"I took my phone off the hook."

"There's a mandatory evacuation. We need to leave now."

"I thought it was turning."

"It looks like it's going to be a Cat 5 and we're right in its path." I looked around one last time at all the stuff I couldn't save. I grabbed pictures of my parents and I threw them all into my little safe that contained my passport, insurance and bank papers (and sadly, my marriage license) and threw it in the back seat of my pick-up truck.

I made arrangements to have my Corvette transported to the other coast to be garaged – I couldn't let anything happen to my car. At the last minute I shoved some of my favorite jewelry into my bag.

I drove my truck and waited in line behind Carol's car, along with all the other residents fleeing the island on Summerlin Road. We drove to the church. It seemed to take forever. Oh well, if we were going to blow away, at least I was with people I knew. We were all stuck only a few miles away from the storm. We waited helplessly while the storm passed us, or ruined us all.

We braved the storm in a huge sanctuary that seemed way too small for all the people crammed into it. Several people had weather radios. We waited for the report to come in. There wasn't good news – Fort Myers Beach was a direct hit.

When the power came back on, I turned on my iPad, to see the damage for myself. There was a guy reporting from the beach. He called Fort Myers Beach 'totally destroyed.' In the following days, conservative estimates put the damage in the billions and only a few towns had been assessed at that point.

I drove back before anyone else. I had to see what had happened to my life. I knew everything was gone. I didn't even wonder, I just knew. When it rains, it pours. I drove over the Matanzas Pass Bridge and had to show my license to get back on the island. It was a different view.

Normally, when you come up the bridge, you notice the ocean. Now, all you noticed was debris. There were trees everywhere. Homes were gone – I mean, down-to-the-foundation gone. I drove by where the diner should have been and knew nothing was going to be the same, even if I re-built it.

The phones lines were out because they were sitting under rubble. The cell towers were down too. Power was still out in certain areas. Everyone was traumatized, standing in line for food and water. I drove to the beach before I drove to Buckingham, where the river house remained unscathed.

I sat on a piece of shredded lumber, screaming to the insurance adjuster on the phone. They were running days late on appointments. The insurance lady told me to wait in my house. "Are you kidding me with that? There *is* no house!" Carol was there with me, but there was nothing anyone could do.

I spent two days sitting on the concrete pad of my house, sweating in the heat and humidity. Finally, I saw a truck pull up and a guy get out. The first thing I noticed was his work boots. I don't know why I kept staring at those boots. Then Carol grabbed my shoulder.

"Megan, what's with you?" she yelled at me.

I looked up at her. "What?"

"Look at the guy *wearing* the work boots." I looked at his face and realized it was not my insurance guy. It was Mark. He started walking towards me.

"Megan," he said quietly. I stood up.

"What are you doing here? The police aren't even allowing people who don't live here on the island."

"Yeah, well, they're fans. I just had to repeat that line from Don O'Malley."

"Oh, the one about not being a 'one woman kind of guy because you're not good at math?'" I asked with a major attitude.

"That's the one. Look, I'm going to Italy on Thursday to shoot that commercial. But I'm getting married first."

Carol looked at me for my reaction, and then turned around and walked away. I could feel my blood pressure rising. I jumped to my feet, my hands balled up into fists at my side.

"How dare you, Mark Taylor! Take a look around, I have lost everything! I thought I lost everything the day you left me. Now, I really have. And you come to gloat." I wanted to smack his face. "Well, good, go and get married to some little hussy."

"Now wait a minute. What are you so angry about?" Then he realized what I was thinking. "Did you hear that I was back with Sophia?"

"Yes I did. You left me and went back to her, you –" I raised my hand to slap him, but he caught hold of my wrist, then turned it and slid his fingers between mine.

"I haven't seen her since the wrap party, Megan. Seriously."

"Then why would they run that story?" I wanted to believe him, but I was too mad.

He laughed. "*Prying Eyes* is opening next weekend. The studio leaked it."

"Why?"

"It's publicity for the movie. The public loves celebrity romances, even if they're concocted. *You*, of all people, should know you can't believe everything you read."

A little bud of hope started growing. "So you're not marrying some little hussy?"

"That depends. Do you think you're a hussy?" He smiled that blinding smile I'd missed so much.

"Yours." I grabbed his t-shirt with my fists. I looked down. "I like your work boots."

"All hussies like work boots." My laugh got caught up on a sob of relief.

Carol came back to us.

Mark looked at her. "Carol, I'd like to get your blessing to marry Megan."

"Please, take her...you have my blessing!" We all laughed.

He kicked some sharp debris away and got down on one knee in the rubble. Carol got her smart phone out and recorded his proposal.

"Megan, I came here to make a movie about the past and I wound up finding my future."

"Wow, that was good." I said.

"It was, wasn't it?" He grinned.

"Will you please do me the honor of being my wife?"

"Forever?" I asked.

"Yes, *forever*."

He stood up and pulled out the little black box his dad gave him out of his pocket and opened it. "It was my grandmother's. My mother told me she wanted me to give it to the woman I marry. She's going to cry when she finds out I gave it to you."

"Ooh, can I tell her?" I almost jumped up and down in my excitement.

"*After* we're married!"

"So, this is not a conflict-free diamond?" I asked.

He chuckled. "No, *definitely* not!" he said.

Mark slid the diamond ring onto my left hand. "I'm sorry it's not bigger."

"I hope I never hear that again." We both laughed.

"You won't, I promise," he said.

"What took you so long?" I asked.

"I had to make sure I couldn't live without you."

"All you had to do was ask me. I knew you couldn't!" I said.

"I love you so much, Megan."

"Can I ask you one thing, Mark? Why did you leave that night? You know…before…you know?"

"Oh, that." He put his arms around me. "God told me to."

"You mean your conscience?"

"Nope. My conscience isn't that loud. There was a terrifying voice telling me not to have sex with you, and thunder and lightning and everything."

"Really?" I looked into his eyes wonderingly, and then remembered something serious.

"Where am I going to live? I don't have a home anymore."

"Oh, Megan, the television pilot I shot was picked up by the network. And it's being filmed in Miami. They've got some really good writers. The show should do well."

"So we're moving to Miami?" Now I *did* jump up and down.

"Yeah, I know of this nice Mediterranean house right on the water..."

"But it doesn't have a music studio."

"No, but I know an architect who could add one!"

I scowled at him. "Is that supposed to be funny?"

"I thought it was."

"Can we get married now?" I asked.

"What about the insurance adjuster? Don't you need to wait?" he asked.

"I have people." I smiled.

"Right. I guess that means now I have people, too?" he looked at me.

"Mm hmm."

He pulled out his phone. "I have to call the airline and have them add you to my flight."

"Um, yeah, too bad I can't afford to charter a jet for us."

He looked up at me. "Oh, right. I'm not used to this."

"You will be," I said.

We called the pastor to officiate. And we already had the license! He was so happy I was getting married. I think his exact words were, 'Yes! Thank the Lord.'

Then I called Joseph Carr and asked if he'd like to be the one to cover the story. He said yes, of course, then, "I heard what you did for me."

"I don't know what you're talking about, Mr. Carr," I

said innocently.

"Candy told me everything, Megan."

"I've never heard you call me anything but 'The Lottery Heiress.'"

"Well, I guess now I'll be calling you Mrs. Taylor!"

I smiled and hung up the phone. Mark drove Carol to the church and they waited for my return. Carol said Bud was going to be there too.

I drove back to the river house so I could shower and change. I tried to find a white dress in my closet. I only had an ivory dress – that was probably more appropriate anyway. The pastor started the ceremony as soon as I got back. Only a handful of people could attend with everything going on.

There were a few church employees there, so we were able to find someone who could play "The Wedding March." As I walked down the aisle, holding Bud's arm, I wondered if my parents could see me. I started to get emotional.

Then I saw Mark standing at the end of that very, very long aisle. I looked to the left, in the front row, to see Joseph Carr standing with his daughter, Liz. She smiled and waved at me and that's when I lost it! We asked for the short version. Carol was crying the whole time!

When Bud handed me off to Mark, Bud kissed my cheek and I just smiled. The ceremony went off without a hitch, until the pastor got to the part where I was supposed to repeat, "I will love and be faithful." I got a case of the giggles when I tried to repeat the word 'faithful.' At first, Mark thought it was cute until I tried the second and third time – then he just got annoyed. I couldn't stop laughing. Mark stopped the ceremony and looked at me.

"Megan? That's *really* not a part you should be laughing at."

"I'm sorry. I promise I won't cheat on you! But, you have to understand... I'm marrying *Mark Taylor,*" and then I giggled again.

Mark looked at the pastor and said, "Just wrap this up, okay?"

From then on, the pastor told me to just nod in response. The whole ceremony took less than five minutes. He pronounced us husband and wife and we kissed. Everyone clapped. Carol came over to us.

"I'm so happy for you, honey. You deserve this!" she said as she hugged me. "Mark, you are a life-saver," she said as she pulled him in for a hug and whispered, "and if you hurt her, I'll bury you next to my *cat!*"

"Don't worry, Carol. I'll take care of her." He smiled at her.

Even Joseph hugged me. "I hope you don't mind I brought Liz."

"Not at all. You've gotten so big, Liz – I hardly recognize you!"

She hugged me.

I'm really happy for you, Mr. and Mrs. Taylor," Joseph said. He shook Mark's hand, "Congratulations, man." Mark smiled and nodded and shook Liz's hand.

What a scoop! Imagine being the only reporter allowed in the ceremony!

Mark looked at me and said we had to leave. He wanted to get to Italy early, since now he would be honeymooning there, as well as shooting a commercial.

Because of the hurricane damage, we couldn't fly out of the Fort Myers airport. We had to fly out of the east coast, which was fine because that meant we could spend the night at The Breakers and fly out of West Palm. I called the hotel and asked for my favorite suite. We waited for the limousine and we started on our journey together.

Mark and I were all over each other in the limo. Finally, I backed off.

"What's the matter?" he asked.

"I'm trying not to have sex with you in a car!"

"I won't judge you!" he said with a mischievous smile.

"C'mon, I don't want our first time to be in a car."

"Fine, keep your hands to yourself until we hit the Palm Beach County line and then we'll start warming up."

I laughed. I still was giggling a little inside that I was married to *Mark Taylor*!

After a few minutes and a really good kiss, I pulled out my phone. "I have to call Cindy. She's going to be upset that she couldn't stand up for me in the ceremony."

"She'll understand," Mark said. I wasn't convinced.

I didn't even say hello when she answered. "So, I wanted to tell you I just married Mark Taylor, before he tweets it." Mark signed on to his Twitter account as I was talking.

I had to hold the phone away from my ear because she was squealing so loudly. I put it on speakerphone. "Why didn't you wait for me?"

"I'm sorry. I knew you were going to be mad!"

"Are you going to have a honeymoon?"

"We're going to Italy in the morning," I said.

"Did you *do* him yet?"

"No, but I'm sure he'll tweet about that too!" Mark smacked my leg and smiled.

"Where are you staying?"

ANGELINA ASSANTI

"The Breakers."

"Oooh. Can I come see you before you go?"

"No, I don't think that's a good idea." I looked at Mark. "I don't think we'll come out of our room until tomorrow."

Mark winked at me. "Hi Cindy," he said loudly into the phone.

"Oh, I'm going to kill you, you didn't tell me I was on speaker. *Hi, Mark!*"

I laughed. "I will call you as soon as we get back from Italy, I promise."

"Yee haw! Get some for me, Megan."

"Goodbye, Cindy."

"She's a really good influence on me," I said sarcastically.

"I can tell."

Mark took my hand and kissed it. "Are you nervous?"

"Not at all."

"Yeah, me neither," he said.

"Actually, I lied. I am a little nervous." I said.

Mark's face relaxed. "I'm glad you are too. It feels like prom night."

"Wow, you must've had a really good prom."

"My girlfriend and I got in a fight and I dropped her off early."

"My boyfriend passed out."

Mark laughed, and then leaned over for another long kiss. "I hope we have a better night than the prom."

Once our driver pulled up, we met our private concierge at the front door, and we just about ran to the elevator and then to the room. We got the Imperial Suite – that's the room I always stay in when I'm there.

There are amazing ocean views from every window –

not that we'd be spending much time admiring the view! I requested some specialty foods be stocked in the kitchen, in case we didn't leave the room.

Mark looked me over, up and down. "Do you want to get some dinner?"

I shook my head as I turned the deadbolt and double-checked it.

He actually seemed nervous, standing there trying to set the date on his watch. I went up to him and kissed him. I led him to the bedroom. I backed him up to the bed. I pushed him down.

"Are you ready for some real Northern Aggression?"

He grinned. "Oh, yes." He didn't seem nervous anymore.

He was incredible. It was very hot. Remember I wondered what kind of lover he would be after watching him in all those movies? Well, let's just say he was a nice mix of all those characters. After that night, I was convinced that he really was made just for me. It was weird – who knew married sex would be so amazing?

I thanked God for making me wait. It was totally worth it. I cannot believe I get to be with this guy every night. Life is good. Well, it *can* be bad. But then it gets better and then you wind up with this smokin' hot guy you never expected.

The next morning I woke up to an empty bed. I heard Mark stirring in the sitting room, making coffee from a cart filled with goodies that had just been wheeled in.

I walked out in my fluffy hotel bathrobe. "Good morning," I said.

"Good morning, Mrs. Taylor." He kissed me.

"Did you sleep okay?" I asked.

"Yes, I very much enjoyed my two hours of sleep."

I laughed. "Sorry."

"I'm just grateful you didn't kill me," he said with a smile and a lingering kiss.

"What time's the limo going to be here?" I asked.

He looked at his watch. "They'll be here in about two hours."

I made a bagel with lox and cream cheese and took a bite. "Oh good, we have time for –"

"Hey, I'm out of commission for a while."

I giggled. "I was just going to say 'a shower.'"

"Phew!" he said. When we boarded the jet, the pilot and flight attendant came out to greet Mark and introduce themselves. They were excited to be flying us to Italy. I took their pictures with my new husband and the flight attendant asked how we met. It was a great flight. Mark and I couldn't stop smiling at each other.

I could not believe how beautiful Italy was. It looks so different from pictures and movies. Mark and I did some shopping and I watched the commercial being filmed, which was so cool. We got to use the car for the whole trip.

The food was different from the Italian restaurants at home, but I loved it. Everything was so fresh. The two weeks flew by.

When we came back, we threw a huge wedding reception at The Ritz-Carlton in Naples. Mark's dad seemed genuinely happy for us. And, I didn't have to spend too much time with Georgia. After she had a good crying fit, and told everyone she could that I had stolen her son away, she claimed she had a migraine and left.

A year passed and I thanked God every day for the blessings he showered on us. Mark's show was in the top ten every week and married life was great. We'd decided not to rebuild the house in Fort Myers Beach, but kept the river house in Buckingham so we could stay there on our visits. I'd given Carol the money to rebuild the diner, and then I gave her the business itself.

She renamed it 'Carol's Place.' Everyone still works at the diner. The only major change since we left is that she and Bud got engaged! I loved living in Miami, and still being close enough to visit the diner and everyone who was like family to me.

Everything was perfect, until I started feeling fatigued and nauseous. I was frantic. I told Mark, "I think I'm dying." Just my luck for something bad to happen when I was finally so happy.

"Have you been watching *Dr. Oz* again?" he asked.

"I'm serious, something is definitely wrong with me."

Mark got the time off to take me to my doctor.

I sat down in Dr. Bergen's office after they ran a battery of tests. "It's serious, isn't it?"

"Quite," he said. I started to cry. "You're six weeks pregnant, my dear."

"What?" I screamed.

Mark jumped up. "Yeah! My dad was an Olympic swimmer. It's in my DNA!"

I sat stupidly in my chair, totally at sea. "What am I going to do with a baby human?"

"Megan, you'll be fine. Every woman has maternal instincts," Dr. Bergen said.

"Have we met?" I asked sarcastically.

Mark took hold of my shoulders. "Honey, it'll be fine. We'll hire a nanny."

"Are you crazy?" I asked, thinking of all the stars that have run off with their nannies.

"I'm sure I can get my mom to move in and help out."

He grinned. I just shook my head.

A few days later, Mark and I were shopping in Miami. As we were coming out of one of the stores, Mark pointed to someone reading a newspaper. "Check that out," he said pointing to the headline. The headline read, "Mark Taylor and Wife Expecting Their First Baby." We smiled at each other. Just then, the man put the paper down and looked at us. It was Phillip!

Mark pointed to my stomach and howled, "I did that." Mark then pointed at Phillip and said, "Good to see you, Phillip!" I waved to him sympathetically. I actually felt bad for him! He didn't even respond to us. There was a much older woman sitting very close to Phillip. You could tell she had money.

She got excited. "Ooh, Phillip, you didn't tell me you knew Mark Taylor. He's even *better* looking in person!" Mark and I both heard him growl at her.

ABOUT THE AUTHOR

Angelina grew up in a small town in Massachusetts. After moving to attend college, Angelina decided to leave the cold behind and remain in Florida. This is her debut novel. She resides in Fort Myers.

Follow her on Twitter at
@lotteryheiress

Email:
angassanti@gmail.com

Visit her on Facebook at
facebook.com/angelinaassanti

Visit her website:
www.thelotteryheiress.com